In this book, my friend Rabbi Daniel Cohen has crafted an intriguing and inspiring read that shows us no matter what the circumstances, we can all find our faith in humanity and in God if we only open up ourselves to the possibilities.

—*Chuck Leavell, keyboardist for the Rolling Stones and the Allman Brothers and founder of Mother Nature Network*

The Secret of the Light is a moving and captivating exploration of the powerful human emotions that must be reconciled with our very personal spiritual boundaries. (It brings to life the force of a young man's dreams, the burden of cultural expectations, and the love we can only recognize through loss.) A must read for anyone in touch with their spirit and in search of their purpose.

—*Rich Vogel, Founding partner Loeb Enterprises*

As a Roman Catholic, I find Rabbi Cohen's sincerity, insight and message transcends age, disposition or faith. Most importantly, there has never been a better moment in time for this type of reflection and dialogue. His writing will provide a small sample of the man himself, and it will change your life.

—*Alfred G. Wilton, web designer*

There isn't a time that I walk away from either speaking with Rabbi Cohen in-person or reading his blog or watching his videos, when I don't feel fuller from the experience. Rabbi Cohen is my first exposure to a Jewish Rabbi and not only am I captivated by his thoughts, I have never felt alienated by virtue of what I believe or by what he has to share. His message is universally uplifting. I feel blessed to have the great fortune of having learned and grown through this man.

—*Nicole Williams, bestselling author, career expert for LinkedIn*

D0898617

THE SECRET OF THE LIGHT

Rabbi Daniel Cohen

UNION SQUARE
PUBLISHING

Published by
Union Square Publishing
301 E 57th Street
4th Floor
New York, NY 10022

Manufactured in the United States of America, or in the
United Kingdom when distributed elsewhere.

    LCCN: 2022917749
    Cohen, Rabbi Daniel
    The Secret of the Light

ISBN: 978-1-946928-30-6
eBook: 978-1-946928-31-3

Cover design by: Joe Potter
Copyediting by: Diane Cohen
Interior design by: Claudia Volkman
Author Photo: Aviva Maller

www.RabbiDanielCohen.com

Dedicated in memory of Ethel and Syril Shraiberg
by Steve and Kay Shraiberg

PART ONE

Caleb is taking the subway to Times Square, as he's done every Sunday night for eight weeks. He's going to the Holiday Inn on 42nd Street just west of Times Square. That's where his prep class for the Law School Admission Test takes place in a gloomy conference room with coffee-stained carpeting and poor ventilation.

In Caleb's mind, it is no wonder the LSAT office is located in this neighborhood. It's Times Square of the 1980s, dirty and wretched. Over decades following World War 2 and affected by the lingering impact of the Great Depression, Times Square is now known as the "the sleaziest block in America." Crime, prostitution and drugs thrived.

He enters the 190th Street station with a book of LSAT sample tests in his hand. A tunnel leads to the elevator that carries riders down to the tracks. Graffiti covers the tunnel's walls, insane lettering illegible in the dim light.

The elevator too has obscene graffiti and there's a strong scent of stale beer. Sometimes there are rats.

Caleb is on the platform. He pulls off his head covering, his kippah, and replaces it with a worn baseball cap. Down the track a train approaches, its light getting brighter and larger like a snake with its head on fire.

He boards the train. Graffiti covers the walls and the

orange plastic seats. The car is half-full on Sunday night. No one is speaking, no eye contact. Caleb finds an open seat as the train lurches forward.

Caleb randomly opens the book of sample tests. He reads:

The town of Nuxhall has 16,400 residents in 1953 and 20,000 residents in 1975. Nuxhall is serviced by three garbage dumps, each of which can accept garbage from 6,000 people per week.

He closes the book and removes a much smaller book from his jacket. It's a copy of the Old Testament, the Tanach, bound in red leather. Caleb can hardly read the tiny print in the subway's uncertain light.

He opens at random to Numbers 23:22. He reads:

God who brought him forth out of Egypt; is for them like the horns of a wild ox . . . a people that rises like a lion.

Every verse in the Bible is important, every word, every letter, and even the white spaces between the letters and words. But the verses need to be correctly understood.

Caleb reflects for a moment on the profound transition that has occurred between his reading the meaningless question in the sample test book and this verse from the book of Numbers. He closes his eyes for a moment in deep thought. As he does so, the meaning of the verse becomes clear.

Everyone struggles to navigate good and evil. Every moment is a choice between our lower and higher angels and

Caleb was no different than anyone. Sometimes we descend to see how far we can rise.

No matter how dark the night, Times Square is always artificially illuminated, just as Egypt was infused with counterfeit pleasures. Standing in the center of the plaza, it is hard to know whether it is day or night. There are few places on earth where the two lights, one real and one not are commingled.

But the Jews went down into Egypt. Why did they go down? The soul is like a muscle. It will atrophy without exercise and will diminish its power if not pushed beyond the limit. Perhaps the Jewish people couldn't achieve their destiny if never enslaved. Maybe, Caleb thinks to himself, he is drawn to Times Square to see how much he can rise.

He looks up. The train has stopped. People are filing out of the car. He has arrived at Times Square.

Caleb is on the corner of Eighth Avenue and 42nd Street. Hundreds of glaring neon signs have changed the night into something artificial, shameful, dangerous. For Caleb it feels tempting but also liberating, just as Egypt was a first step toward liberation.

Caleb drops his LSAT workbook into a trash bin and walks east on 42nd Street. Immediately a man wants to sell him a watch. Another sidles up beside him mumbling, "Smoke? Smoke?" Caleb ignores them. He walks a full block, then crosses the street and heads back toward Eighth Avenue.

He tightens his scarf around his neck. The street is bright as day, but this is the darkest place in America, he philosophizes. The movie theaters, the porn shops, the peep shows, he indifferently passes them by. He's testing himself. He pulls off his cap and dons his head covering again as if in triumph for resisting the temptations. He keeps his hat at the ready in case he is lured back in. Just as everything in life is a reprise of the Torah narrative, everything in life is a test.

At the corner he moves away from the Port Authority building and then walks north on Eighth Avenue. This is different. No crowds here, no more bright lights, no movie houses. Pizza joints instead, bars, liquor stores.

Another man jumps out of a doorway. He too wants to sell Caleb a watch. Caleb brushes past the man and reaches the corner of 43rd Street. Looking down 43rd Street is like looking into a hole. The street is dark and deserted though only a block from Times Square.

He starts down 43rd Street. He enters that deep hole. He wants a twinge of danger to challenge himself with a real test, not the annoying LSAT his father has tried to impose on him. And what a waste of time that prep class has been, a distraction, not a real test.

"I haven't seen you here before . . ."

Caleb turns quickly. Another watch seller? No, this man looks very different. Certainly an odd-looking man, neither old nor young, wearing a knee-length canvas coat, a faded New York Yankees baseball cap, and holding a long-handled broom. But he seems friendly enough, with a wry smile on his face.

"I haven't been here before," Caleb replies.

The man nods. "Well, there's a first time for everything, as the saying goes. This may seem like an odd question but would you like to join me for a cup of tea? I'm a street sweeper—self-appointed, by the way—but I've swept enough for one night. Are you of the Jewish faith?"

"Yes, I am."

"How did I know that? It must be the *kippah* you're wearing. Very few non-Jews wear them," he laughs. "I myself never go uncovered before the Lord. Come on, let's have a cup of tea. Or seltzer water if you prefer."

"Seltzer water?"

"Jews love seltzer water, or they used to. It was sold from push carts on Hester Street on the Lower East Side. That was only about seventy years ago."

The man steps around Caleb and begins unlocking a heavy wooden door with a Star of David carved in its center. If not for this encounter with the street sweeper, Caleb would have missed the carving in the darkness. He's surprised by its weather-beaten artistry. He's even more surprised to see something like this on 43rd Street.

The street sweeper opens the door with a gallant gesture. "Please come in!"

Caleb hesitates. "Can you tell me your name?"

"Elijah."

"I'm Caleb."

"Follow me."

With the door unlocked, Caleb follows Elijah inside. They enter a single large room, sparsely furnished but with a warm ambience. A small candle flickers on a table stacked with books. This is a scholarly street sweeper.

"Please sit down," Elijah says.

Caleb settles into a worn armchair beside the table as Elijah prepares two cups of tea. As Caleb dutifully recites the blessing before taking a sip, Elijah suddenly chimes in: "Baruch Hu! Blessed is God!" and at the end he proclaims, "Amen!"

But he looks serious as he sits down across from Caleb.

"I'm curious about what brought you to Times Square tonight."

"My father is a lawyer, and he wants me to be a lawyer too. He got me a job in a law firm. I know he wants me to make a good living but I have serious doubts about the merits and quite frankly the meaning of devoting my life to it. I've been going to the Holiday Inn on Tenth Avenue every Sunday night for a prep class for the Law School Admission Test. Tonight I couldn't face that even one more time."

"I see. Was there a textbook for the class?"

"Yes, there was."

"Did you throw it in a trash can?"

"Actually, I did. How did you know that?"

"Well, as a street sweeper I've looked in a lot of trash cans. You're not the first one who threw that book away. But I don't think the class is the only reason you're in Times Square. There must be some dark side that you feel the need to serve or at least explore inside yourself. Am I right about any of that?"

"I was raised in an observant Jewish home and I'm following the path laid out for me by my family. To be honest, growing up my parents instilled in me a faith in God. I recited prayers morning and night, blessings before and after eating but over time the words lacked meaning for me. I was just going through the motions. I'm doing my best but sometimes I feel conflicted. People I respect have tried to strengthen me in my faith and I'm grateful for that. When I come down here it's such a different world. In Times Square I just feel like . . ."

"You don't really know how you feel," Elijah interrupts. "Coming to Times Square isn't the right thing for a *boychik* to be doing, but you're drawn to it for that same reason. You think this is a forbidden place, a dark place, and you're right. That's an attraction. But it's also an opportunity to bring in light. Good things *can* happen here. We can do that in Times Square, and we can do the same thing in our own souls."

Caleb smiles. "Is that your bar mitzvah speech?"

"Very funny! Meanwhile, besides trying to be a lawyer because your father wants you to, is there any excitement in your life? Do you have a girlfriend?"

"No, not right now."

"Not right now? What does that mean? Have you ever had a girlfriend?"

Without waiting for a reply, Elijah takes a book from the stack on the table and places it in front of him. Caleb can read the title that's printed in gold letters on the cover: *The Secret of the Light.*

Elijah says, "The secret of the light is the secret of life itself. For centuries it's been known by the sages of kabbalah, the greatest work of mysticism. Someday, when everyone lives their lives according to the secret of the light, that's when the Messiah will come. But just as the Tree of Knowledge was forbidden in the Garden of Eden, access to the Secret has to be earned."

"But is the secret in that book?

"It certainly is."

"How is it a secret then? The book is right here on the table."

Elijah shakes his head. "It's not that simple. When you walk past a bank, there's a lot of money in there. It's very close. But to get that money you have to own it. You have to earn it. It's the same way with this book."

Caleb isn't sure what to make of this. Elijah seems sincere, but what he's saying is pretty far out.

"Who is the author of the book?"

"He's called the Reb. His name doesn't matter."

"The Reb?"

Suddenly Elijah's manner changes. It seemed like they were going to have a long talk. Now he seems distracted, rushed.

"It's getting late, Caleb," Elijah says, standing up from his chair, "I think you should head home now."

Caleb is confused, but he also stands. "Okay . . . ."

Elijah leads the way across the room. "Come back whenever you like and we can continue to talk."

He opens the door. "But there's one thing I want you to know right now."

Caleb is still startled by Elijah's change in mood. "What do you want me to know?"

"I want you to know that your real discoveries won't be with me. They'll be made in Israel."

"Israel?"

But Elijah, the street sweeper, seems to sweep Caleb out the door and back onto 43rd Street.

Has this really happened? It seems so unreal to Caleb. But the door with the Star of David is still there. He hears the sound of a lock.

Caleb works in midtown, but he lives in an apartment on Bennett Avenue in northern Manhattan. It's near Fort Tryon Park, not far from Yeshiva University where he'd gone to college. It's an affordable two-bedroom that he shares with Jessie, his classmate at Yeshiva.

The apartment is empty when Caleb returns from Times Square. Jessie is still at his parents' place. He's gone home for shabbat.

Caleb opens the door to his darkened bedroom and sees the red light blinking on his answering machine. He assumes it's his father calling about some insignificant concern. That often happens. And Caleb is partly right. It's a message from Sam but it's not an insignificant concern.

What Caleb hears takes his breath away. "You've got to come right now to the Weill-Cornell hospital on York Avenue. There's a problem with your mother. A very serious problem."

Caleb rushes out of the apartment, runs at top speed to Broadway. It isn't late yet; there are plenty of cabs. Caleb flags one down and gives the driver the name of the hospital.

Bouncing along in the back seat of the taxi, Caleb feels uncertain about everything. Did he actually meet a scholar of kabbalah in Times Square tonight? Was there really a book that explained everything? Who was the Reb? And most importantly, did he really get a panicked phone message from his father? Is that why he's riding in this taxi?

At York Avenue, he gives the driver a generous tip and jumps out of the cab.

Somehow, he knows she's going to die.

On the fourth floor of the hospital adjacent to the Neurocritical Intensive Care unit there's a waiting room with plastic seats like those on the subway. Fluorescent ceiling lights reflect off the linoleum floor and off walls decorated with magnifications of neurons and brain cells.

Caleb is out of breath when he finds this place in the

hospital complex, and what he sees isn't reassuring. A few seats are occupied by worried family members of ICU patients. Among them are Sam and Uncle Maish, his mom's older brother. They're staring blankly across the room, but they spring to their feet when Caleb enters.

"Thank God you're here," Maish says. "It was an aneurysm. Out of nowhere."

"Out of nowhere," Sam repeats. "She was standing in the living room and the next minute she was on the floor. I called 911. The doctor says there are usually warning signs. But who knows?"

Caleb is overwhelmed, speechless. From the depths of his soul he asks, "Did you pray? We have to pray."

"Of course we prayed!" Maish snaps but immediately regrets his angry response.

For Caleb there are so many questions: Where is she now? When can I be with her? When can I talk to her?

In college Caleb spoke with Sam every week or so. But Elyse, his mom, seemed to be present at every moment. In the summers when he was at camp, there was a call every few days. She also sent him letters in her beautiful handwriting. He would write back, although not as promptly as he should have.

Even over the phone he could feel her smile and her zest for life. He could talk with her about anything. She would listen to him and love him and encourage him to do his best with his God-given talents. Regardless of any problems she was facing, she always said, "Thank God, I'm doing fantastic!"

Caleb experiences a flashback. From a very young age, when Caleb would leave the house his mom would say to him two things.

"Caleb, never forget who you are and never forget whose you are. You are a child of God." Her loving reminder anchored him and served as a lighthouse in his life.

Would he ever hear those words again? Tears are welling up in his eyes. In the darkest storms of everyday life, she could break through the clouds with hope and light.

In the waiting room Caleb falls into the numb and passive state shared by everyone there.

He tries to resist it. "Is there anything we can do?"

Sam shrugs. "What can we do? When the doctor comes out maybe we'll get some information."

"What about Nora?" Caleb asks. Nora is his ten-year-old sister.

"She's with Amanda and Glenn," Sam says, referring to his neighbors in the apartment building on 107th Street. "I told them what happened and that we'd probably be late. If we're lucky Nora is asleep."

Caleb has more questions but no energy to ask. It isn't nine o'clock yet, but the waiting room is like a bus station at midnight.

Maish can't handle the silence. He says, "There's a Midrash where the rabbis argue about who's the most beautiful woman in the Torah."

"I've never heard of anything remotely like that," Sam says. He sounds offended.

"I certainly couldn't make it up." Maish's voice is trembling. "Do you think this is some triviality, Sam? Obviously, the rabbis weren't talking about physical beauty. They meant the kind of spiritual beauty that can only exist in women who are high souls. My sister Elyse is a woman like that. Elyse is a very high soul!"

He's sobbing, and then he's apologetic. "I'm sorry. I was just trying to make conversation."

Across the room a door opens and a woman in a physician's white coat enters the waiting room. It's the doctor. As a reflex, Caleb assesses whether she's Jewish. He decides that she is and feels reassured, but only slightly. As she approaches he reads the name embroidered on her coat: C. Lander, M.D.

Sam introduces Caleb and the doctor smiles. "I'm Carla. Let's go to the conference room."

In the hallway Dr. Lander unlocks the door of a small room furnished with a round table, three chairs, and a potted plant in one corner. There are no windows. When the doctor flips the switch the room turns artificially bright.

Ignoring chairs, the three men huddle around the doctor like children eager to be fed. Dr. Lander is used to this. Her voice is calm.

"I wish I had good news, but I don't. Elyse has a severe bleed. Her signs are dropping. I'm sorry."

Silence follows, stunned, painful, intolerable. The doctor adds, "There's a severe neurologic deficit. Her brain is showing rapid global atrophy."

This is a foreign language, but they get the general idea. Maish asks, "What do we do now?"

The doctor says, "In this hospital we have a compassionate, family-centered approach to patient care. We keep patients' loved ones informed of a patient's medical status. We absolutely include family members in decision-making."

But this doesn't really answer the question. Sam is on an entirely different frequency. He says, "How can this possibly be happening?"

"I know you want to be with her now," says the doctor as she turns back toward the door.

In an Intensive Care cubicle with Sam and Maish, Caleb sees Elyse on the bed amid a dozen wires and softly beeping devices. How can she suddenly be so sick? It doesn't make sense. She looks peaceful and even young, her dark hair stylishly short and brushed to one side, her breathing calm but shallow.

Yet he knows she's going to die. He'll never speak to her again. His only chance is if, by accepting her death, maybe her death won't happen. It's like waving a white flag and hoping for mercy from the enemy.

He squeezes his mother's hand. She holds his hand tightly, or so it seems. He isn't sure. Is she going to leave him now? Can she still be present in his life even when she's physically absent?

What about God? Is God here and not here at the same time? Right now that sounds very unconvincing.

Caleb feels entirely lost. Maish and Sam are on either side of him holding on to his arms. It's a lot of weight, as if they're trying to drag him down. He doesn't feel like supporting the two grown men. Sam is trying to recite a psalm: "Though I walk in the valley of the shadow of death I will fear no evil, for you are with me . . ."

The words seem empty to Caleb. If God is with us, why is this happening to his mom? Hundreds of times he's recited verses of the psalms, but he never really thought about them. Now he wants them to be true, but he can't find light in them. The veil is too thick, the pain too raw and deep. He feels surrounded by darkness.

The doctor is leaving. Maish pulls away from Caleb. He says, "Thank you so much for everything, doctor."

She nods. "If you need anything I'll be here."

"We'll be here too," Maish adds, "and I really can't thank you enough."

Maish is emotional as he rejoins Sam and Caleb. "Oh my God, Oh my God," he repeats.

Caleb sees what's happening with alarming clarity. He sees that this is the last two minutes of his mother's life. The last minute. Then the final seconds.

He holds her hand and whispers the six-word affirmation that is the foundation of the Jewish faith. Speaking these words at the end of your life is supposed to be a supreme blessing. Caleb has little patience for all that now, but he knows his mother would have done it herself if she could. Now he does it for her.

He whispers, *"Sh'ma Yisrael, Hashem Elokeinu, Hashem echud." Hear O Israel, the Lord our God, the Lord is One.*

To his surprise and everlasting comfort, he feels his mother lightly squeeze his hand. Her eyes are closed but he knows he is not imagining. He whispers, "Mom, don't let go. I already miss you so much."

Caleb remembers an early teaching: every human being comes into this world with hands clenched and leaves the world with hands wide open. It symbolizes the journey and challenge of life. The mark of a successful life is learning to move from selfishness to selflessness. Life is about love and unconditional giving. His mom has given her heart and soul to him. She is leaving with her hands and heart fully open.

Her touch awakens a flood of memories: holding his

mother's hand at the zoo, walking to synagogue, combing his hair, hugging him before he leaves for camp, everything flashes before him.

Then he feels a sudden change. She releases his hand and her hands open and fall to her side. It's as if his hand is on the side of a warm toaster when the cord is disconnected from the wall. The temperature suddenly changes. He will never forget it.

With Caleb at her bedside, his mom, the foundation of his life and of their family, takes her last breath. Now he feels like he's living in two worlds: one of hope and one of despair.

But can this really be happening? Where is God now? Does he still believe? Can he still believe?

Maish uses a car service that drives him around the city in a big Lincoln. In the intensive care unit, he uses the phone at the nurses' station for the driver to pick him up outside the hospital. Sam's car is in the underground parking area.

Riding silently in the elevator with Sam and Maish is one of the most difficult experiences of Caleb's life.

The elevator arrives at the ground floor and the door opens. "I'll see you in the morning," Maish says, and gets off.

Caleb and Sam keep going to the parking level. To Caleb, all this procedure seems unreal and also insensitive at the same time.

Finally Sam and Caleb are in the car on the Manhattan streets.

Sam is behind the wheel. He's not a careful driver. At the risk of unnerving him Caleb says, "The doctor told me we should call a mortuary."

"No. She'll go directly to Israel. I've already spoken to a guy about that. He has a company that handles it."

Caleb is shocked. "Israel?"

"That's right. Your mom has got to be buried as soon as possible, and it's going to happen in Israel."

At first that seems impossible to Caleb. Then he remembers the day—he was eleven or twelve years old—when he sat in his father's home office and Sam said, "I want to speak with you about something that you'll have to deal with someday, but not for a long time, God willing. I've purchased graves for your mother and me in Israel."

But Caleb can't remember the subject ever coming up again until now. How will his mother be transported to Israel so quickly? What will the casket be like? What will happen at the funeral?

Even thinking about practical matters seems like an insult to his mother's memory. Staring out the window of the Lincoln, Caleb can't release the image of his mother lying motionless in the hospital. Doesn't he owe it to her to keep this memory alive? He'd like to remember her vibrant smile, but now her lifeless image occupies his every thought.

They ride in silence as the car passes through Central Park. It's dark now, a cold night is coming. On nights like this Sam had always reminded Caleb to go with him to the synagogue for the evening service. Caleb had always gone, not understanding what the prayers meant but appreciating their importance. Now, as mourners, Jewish tradition exempts them from prayers. Their only concern should be the funeral for his mother and the other obligations to honor her.

On Broadway, Sam pulls into the garage where he has rented a space for three decades. Sam and Elyse had lived on the Upper West Side for years before Caleb was born. So much time, and now so many questions. Who will call the family's friends? What about all the religious protocols? Caleb remembers learning that a person's soul will only be at peace once the body returns to the earth. All of a sudden these things become so important. What is the correct way to dress? Who will be providing food during the *shiva*, the week of mourning?

Sam turns off the engine, looks at his watch, and says, "We have to be prepared for tomorrow. The service will be in the morning."

"Didn't you say the funeral is going to be in Israel?" Caleb asks.

"There will be a service here, and then the funeral will be in Israel. Let's get Nora."

Glenn and Amanda Roberts, Sam's neighbors, live in an apartment on the tenth floor down the hall from Sam's. But Glenn and Amanda are comparatively new to the area. They're a couple in their early thirties who had bought the apartment right after their marriage a number of years ago. Amanda had became pregnant shortly after arriving, and it turned out that Nora was born at almost the same time as Lily, the Roberts' daughter. The girls have been best friends ever since.

Glenn answers Sam's knock on the door. Seeing that Sam looks stricken, he shakes his head sadly.

"She's gone?"

"I'm afraid so."

"That's terrible, Sam. Just terrible."

"Yes . . . yes."

Glenn turns to Caleb. "I'm so sorry," he says. "She was such a wonderful woman."

Now Amanda appears with Nora fast asleep on her shoulder. One look tells her what's happened. With great solemnity she passes the sleeping child to Sam.

As she usually does, Amanda skips the small talk. She gives Caleb a nod and a sad smile, then says to Sam, "It's so terrible. How are you going to tell her?"

She means, what is Sam going to say to Nora about Elyse's death? Before he can think of an answer, Amanda advises, "Kids actually know a lot more about death than we think. They see it in cartoons and movies. You don't have to introduce the concept. But why did Elyse die and why so suddenly?"

Caleb turns to Amanda and adds, "Maybe we don't know why. Maybe we never will."

Maish can't sleep. He never drinks but if there was alcohol in his apartment he would be tempted. Elyse's life has ended, and he feels like his own life is ending. It's just a matter of time.

The truth is, he's felt down for the past few years. But now a new level has been reached. What can he look forward to? Is life only going to get worse? Or maybe it will suddenly end, as it did for Elyse.

Over the years, when he was having a bad night, Maish cheered himself up by writing advertising copy for his business. Keeping the ads up to date is important because the business is time-sensitive. For example, if an ad runs in the October issue of a Fraternal Order of Police monthly magazine, it needs to mention the discounted price which the buyer will get if the order is submitted before Thanksgiving. But tonight writing ad copy isn't enough for Maish to calm down. His little sister is gone. From when they were children, she has been the most important woman in his life. In fact, she is the only important woman. Maish has never seriously considered marriage. Everyone jokes that he is married to his business. He rarely attends synagogue if only on Yom Kippur and only then for the memorial prayer of Yizkor. The death of his sister is a blow to his gut and hurts immensely. What's most hurtful is how her death causes him to question for one of the first times the value of his own life.

It's eight in the morning when Caleb, Sam, and Maish arrive at the synagogue. Along with the friends of Elyse who have been notified, they enter the sanctuary and take seats at the front.

Nora is here too, wearing her best dress and looking very puzzled. Sam and Caleb had an intense discussion about whether Nora should attend the service. Would she be frightened? Would she be traumatized? What will she think is going on if she's there? But what will she think if she's not there? Finally they agree that, since Nora isn't going to Israel, it's best if she attends the service.

What a shock it is to see the casket at the front of the room, just ahead of the ark that contains two Torah scrolls.

A side door opens, and Rabbi Kahn enters from his office next to the sanctuary where the funeral is taking place. He's known Elyse's family for many years, as he knows all the families in the congregation. Occasions like this are a frequent part of the rabbi's work. It isn't easy. Rabbi Kahn looks somber; yet this is the work he is called to do.

Sometimes Caleb has felt this calling or thinks he has. But today he feels differently. How can faith in God coexist with what has happened to Elyse? She was only in her early forties.

Rabbi Kahn walks slowly toward Caleb and his family and asks them to rise. In a quiet voice he says, "With all our hearts, we wish we weren't here today. I can only imagine the pain. We pray that God will give you strength in this moment. We will never understand why Elyse, your mother, wife, and sister, died but we affirm that we maintain our faith in God. Through the honor we will give her today and the burial of her vessel, her body, her soul will be at peace and she will continue to live with God and each and every one of us. We begin the service today with the rending of our garments. The Hebrew word is *keriah*."

The rabbi continues: "Even when we're deep in grief, as we are now, we will affirm our belief in God. Judaism teaches that life is complicated. We can be sad, we can be devastated, we can even be angry at God, but we still acknowledge our belief. We are not alone. God walks with us through the valley of the shadow of death. Elyse's soul will live forever."

Nora tugs on Caleb's sleeve. "Is she dead or alive?"

"I'll explain later," Caleb whispers, although internally doubting his resolve and wavering between faith and doubt.

Rabbi Kahn takes a razor blade and makes a small cut in Caleb, Nora, Sam and Maish's clothing. He continues: "Please recite the following blessing and then tear your clothes. Blessed is the Lord of our God Who is the true Judge." The rabbi nods, the family recites the blessing, and the family members begin expanding the rips in their outer garments. Most of the mourners seem to understand exactly how to do this. They're older than Caleb. They've done it before. Caleb turns to Nora to assist her as she looks at him with her weary eyes set into her forlorn face.

Caleb knows this ritual has its foundation in the sacred

writings, but now it only seems like a mechanical exercise. It frightens him to feel this way about religious observance. It angers him too. He's angry that he's distracted from grieving for his mother.

The rabbi then recites the Twenty-Third Psalm in Hebrew. He explains that our greatest honor is to speak lovingly about Elyse, for she is alive in spirit and will hear our words. It is a way to inspire people to emulate her ways and give her strength as she makes the journey to the next world.

Sam speaks in tribute to Elyse, as does Maish. Then it's Caleb's turn. He begins with uncertainty, struggling to find words, but then discovers an inner strength he did not know he had:

Mom always reminded me to count my blessings. She showed me how to look for the good in life. Her love was unconditional. Once I came home from school with a grade that was below average, and she lovingly motivated me to learn from the experience and grow through it. Just her simple letters to me when I was at camp, letting me know what was going on at home each day, lifted me up and eased my homesickness. She gave me her time, she listened to me, she guided me, and I will always miss her love. She is the cornerstone of our family. I know she will always be with us, but I miss her and love her so much.

The eulogies are followed by *Kel Maleh Rachamim*, the traditional prayer for the soul of the departed. Caleb and his family walk beside Elyse as she is carried to the hearse for the next stage of her journey.

Nora has been to the airport before but not like this. The grown-ups are crying like children. It's scary and confusing, different from anything she's seen before. But the scariest part is how Nora feels that she herself is different now. She doesn't have a mother.

Nora holds Caleb's hand as they walk through the airport. At the boarding gate, Sam hugs Caleb and Maish. He hugs Nora with tears in his eyes. "I'll call you. I love you," he says, and boards the plane. It's as though they're seeing him off on a long-awaited vacation to Israel, which is exactly what the families of other passengers are doing. But Sam is leaving on a different kind of journey. It's one of the saddest moments of Sam's life and all of their lives.

The week-long period of mourning known as *shiva*, normally begins after burial of the deceased relative. But for Caleb, Nora, and Maish, *shiva* will begin at the moment that the plane is out of view. They're waiting at the floor-to-ceiling window beside the boarding gate, which is now closed and locked. The nose of the plane is literally only a few yards away. Caleb is dreading the disappearance of the plane, which will mean saying goodbye to his mother forever.

But at this moment of darkest despair, a light unexpectedly arises. The plane is beginning to back away from the gate when Caleb realizes that the pilot is looking directly at him. He cannot believe it. And then the pilot gives Caleb a reassuring smile and a little wave. Perhaps it's his way of saying that Elyse is in good hands and she'll be well taken care of. *That reassurance takes the pilot only a few seconds, but a fleeting gesture can make an eternal difference.* Caleb thinks back that it is exactly what Elijah said: there are always opportunities to reveal the light. And sometimes—often—moments of great difficulty are the greatest opportunities of all.

During *shiva*, friends and relatives come to pay their respects. Caleb receives them in the living room of the apartment where he grew up, though the apartment seems a strange place now. How can it be home if his mother is both there and not there? Memories of her are everywhere, yet she is nowhere to be seen.

Visitors to a *shiva* are supposed to remain silent until the family members speak. This tradition of silence implies that no words can express the intensity of the family's grief or offer solace. But in the modern world it's hard for people to remain quiet. Most sit glumly beside Caleb on the sofa and whisper, "I'm so sorry, she was a wonderful woman." Often there are tears, and sometimes mournful laughter.

Maish is always present at the *shiva*, and sometimes Nora also appears. Sam calls from Israel right after the service at the cemetery. He'll be returning to New York immediately.

"It seems like it all went well," Caleb tells Maish.

"The cemetery is a few miles outside Jerusalem, right?"

"It's in Safed," Caleb says. "Sam says it's a beautiful place. He says he can feel the holiness."

Then Nora speaks up. She says to Caleb, "It was my impression you would explain to me how Mom can be dead and alive at the same time."

Maish is impressed by Nora's ability to express herself. "She talks like an adult!"

"Mom was always reading to her, and Nora likes to read by herself too."

It had seemed to Elyse that Nora was bored by children's

books. When Nora was six years old, Elyse had begun reading Jane Austen novels to her. Nora had loved hearing her mom read, and she also picked up phrases like, "It was my impression."

Caleb says to Nora, "Suppose you use a candle to light another candle. If the first candle goes out, the light it brought to the second candle is still there. Her light is always alive in everything she touched."

Nora is thinking about this. "So her light is still there but she isn't there."

"Well, she's there in her light."

Nora doesn't seem especially satisfied, but at least she has something to think about. "I'm going to my room," she says, and leaves.

Caleb is surprised to hear himself talking about this. He has never really thought about light in spiritual terms or the relationship between light and darkness. Maybe this comes from listening to Elijah? Can ideas be contagious?

During *shiva*, Caleb finds comfort in the presence of his roommate Jessie. As the whirlwind of visitors continues, Jessie walks in the first afternoon after the funeral.

He walks through the door which is always left unlocked in a *shiva* home so visitors can enter at ease but also as a way not to trouble the mourner to answer the door and offer greetings. Jessie has been to Caleb's home numerous times. They have been friends since elementary school and share a love of basketball, all sports actually, and strong loyalty to family.

Jessie peers into the living room and makes eye contact with Caleb as an old friend of his mom is reciting the traditional words of comfort as she gets up to leave. Upon seeing Jessie, Caleb begins to get up.

"Caleb, you sit . . . I cannot tell you how sorry I am."
He walks over to Caleb.

"Man, I just have to get up to give you a hug. This is a nightmare."

Caleb rises. All of a sudden, tears well up. He gives Jessie a firm handshake and a quick pat on the back.

Jessie empathetically says, "I understand. You spoke movingly about your mom at the funeral yesterday, but I cannot imagine the pain you are going through."

Jessie waits for Caleb to sit in his low chair, a sign of mourning, and he takes a seat next to Caleb.

"How are your dad and sister?"

"Nora is struggling as we all are. I feel even worse for her as she is so young and wonder what memories she will have of my mom. She asked me about what happens after death. I did my best to explain to her what I know but recognize that there is so much we do not know about the soul and afterlife."

"Caleb, I get it. My uncle Josh died a few years ago. I sometimes wonder where he is, but I do feel his presence. Did I ever tell you about my uncle and flying a kite?"

"No but what are you talking about?" Caleb asked with curiosity.

"It's about the tug."

Jessie continued, "Remember flying kites when we were kids? We both love when the kites fly as high as they can."

Caleb knowingly smiles.

"I loved flying kites with my Uncle Josh. He was never married, and he adopted us as his own. He once purchased a new kite for me, pastels on the wings, two eyes and the shape of a butterfly. I will never forget the joy of seeing the kite lifted by the wind as I unwound the twine. 'Catch the wind,' he would say. 'You can feel the wind even though you cannot see it.' I ran faster and ever so slowly the kite soared higher until finally it disappeared behind the clouds.

"Uncle Josh asked me, 'Do you feel the tug?'

"'Of course,' I told him.

"He told me, 'You cannot see the kite, but you know it's there!'"

Caleb understands in that moment what Jessie is telling him as he holds back some tears.

"Caleb, I am not sure about the right words for you. I will always be here for you but I do believe that your mom will always be with you. You will feel her tug . . . just always hold on tight to her. You may not see her, but you will feel her presence. Like the wind which you cannot see but you can feel, she is here and like the tug of the kite, she will always be with you."

"Thanks, brother. I am honestly not sure how I will make it each day but God willing, we will somehow find the way. Your words are comforting. My dad, as you know, went to Israel for the burial. Not sure how he is doing but he hopes to be back late tonight so we can all sit *shiva* together."

"How is your mom, Jessie?" Caleb asks.

"She is good. I know she really admired yours."

Caleb mournfully reflects, "I know. Listen, I realize you don't take her for granted but I just wish I had one more hug from mine. Let her know how much you appreciate her. It is crazy. How in one minute here and then…"

"Caleb, it's alright. I will. Always here for you. I hope to see you soon."

"Thanks, buddy."

The pause in visitors lasts about ten minutes and then another stream of people enters the apartment. Caleb and Jessie exchange goodbyes. For Caleb, the visit from Jessie lifts just a bit the heaviness in his heart if only for a day.

Sam returns from Israel that night. When he arrives from the airport, he sits with Caleb and Maish in the living room. Nora has gone to bed.

Sam says, "Right before I left I went to Mom's grave. Then I visited the grave of Rav Isaac Luria. Quite a long line there. He was known as the holy lion."

Caleb says, "I think that has something to do with the Hebrew letters of his name."

"Well, here's another thing that might interest you. It turns out that Safed is quite an artist's colony. Are you familiar with Yehoshua Gips, Caleb?

"No, I'm not."

Sam is obviously energized by what he's about to relate. It's good to see him coming to life. "This is a man, thirty-five or forty at the most, and he's taking the art world by storm. I was walking down a really narrow street in Safed—they're all narrow, but this was really narrow—and a kind of eccentric-looking fellow was coming the other way. He was wearing old blue jeans and a Grateful Dead t-shirt but with a *kippah* and a beard like a Hasid. I knew right away he was an artist because nobody else could look like this. Anyway, we almost bumped into each other because the street was so narrow. I told him that my wife just died, and he very kindly invited me to his studio. It turns out that all his artwork is Hebrew letters. That's all he does. The letters of the Hebrew alphabet!"

But Caleb isn't really surprised that an artist would use the letters as his exclusive subject. He says, "The letters of the Torah are sacred. In the Torah even the white spaces between the letters are sacred."

Maish is listening in. He interrupts, "How can white spaces be sacred?"

But now Sam has something else on his mind. He looks intently at Caleb and says, "I know the hour is late and we need to get to bed, but on the plane ride home I had a lot of time to think. I want you to understand something about Yehoshua Gips. This man's art is Hebrew letters, and he's able to make a good living at it. He's able to be an artist and a businessman at the same time. One doesn't have to detract from the other. Do you know what I'm saying?"

"You're saying I should be a lawyer."

"Well, yes."

"Do we have to talk about this now?"

"We are not actually talking about it, I just wanted to make a point. Please just think about it."

Caleb lifts his hand to tighten the yarmulka on his head and makes sure it is on correctly. Subconsciously, it may be his way of telling his dad he is skeptical of infusing the cutthroat legal world with any semblance of spirituality. In Caleb's mind, he cannot imagine the worlds coexisting in his life—it is more like a collision.

By the last day of *shiva* there is still a stream of visitors, but the number begins to slow down. Sam, Caleb, Nora, and Maish take a walk around the block.

The walk is yet another tradition, a symbolic re-entry into the world, an expression of healing and resilience. But as the door to the house closes behind him for the walk, Caleb feels loneliness like never before, as if he is leaving his mother behind forever.

Winter

In the wake of his mom's tragic passing, Caleb feels as if he is in a trance. Going through the motions. Finding a routine. Morning and evening to services to recite the memorial prayer of Kaddish in honor of his mom, drifting in and out of work late in the morning and early to leave and the coffee and bar breaks to book end and interrupt the day. It is so hard for him to focus and his mind and heart wanders. The effects of his mom's passing are spiritual, emotional, and even physical.

Caleb sees everything in a different light. Yes, he has been observant throughout his life. He has had a bar mitzvah, he keeps kosher, he wears his head covering, dons the *tzitzit fringes*, and puts on *tefillin*, the *phylacteries*, and prays every day. But if he had ever had any doubts about his faith, now it seems like more than just doubt. His mother's death has awakened him to that fact. Having never experienced tragedy, he like most people never really questioned God. He had lived on autopilot, going through the motions of religious life with sporadic emotional intensity.

His only brush with death had been as a child. He was only eight years old. The scene is still vivid in his mind. The memory is etched in his heart as one of sadness but also ironically hope.

"Dad, do you think this will be the last time I will see Grandpa?" Caleb asked his father.

"Caleb, I do not know, but I know Grandpa will be happy to see you."

Caleb and his dad arrived at the entrance to the hospital.

"Caleb, wait here. As an eight year old, you are not allowed up in the patient's room so I will bring Grandpa down in the elevator for you to see him."

Caleb waited anxiously in the lobby of Bronxville Hospital.

The elevator door opened and the moment Caleb feared arrived. Standing behind his grandfather who was seated in a wheelchair, Caleb's Dad motioned for him to walk into the elevator for a final goodbye. His father pressed a button to keep the doors ajar.

They held in place and stood frozen in time.

"Caleb, we only have a couple of minutes yet eternity is in the palm of our hands." For the typical child these words would have been odd but not for Caleb whose father made it a habit to remind him of the gift of every experience and the power of every moment.

Yet Caleb wished time could just stand still. One more hug, one more hour . . . his heart grew heavy.

Slowly, his father pulled out a small book from inside his pants pocket. It was frayed from use and contained Hebrew writing on it. He flipped open to a page and whispered a few words as Caleb walked closer. Caleb's father, Sam, rarely cried but he could see his eyes welling up and a few tears streaming down his face.

As he walked towards his grandfather, Caleb saw that he had a tube underneath his nose to assist with his belabored breathing. He noticed the indentation underneath his grandfather's nose. He never really noticed it before, but it seemed more pronounced this time. Without thinking, Caleb touched his own indentation. He had never really paid much attention to it before, but seeing his grandfather's and then feeling his own awakened a light inside and a small measure of comfort . . . he did not understand why, but he sensed something real fluttering deep in his soul.

Entering the elevator, Caleb hugged and kissed his elderly grandfather. His frail grandfather kissed him back and whispered softly some words into his ear. They were words that would live within him forever. Words that transcended time and space. . . . Tamid . . . Tamid . . . Always . . .

He then placed his hand on Caleb's head and offered a prayer. Angels . . . surrounding and guiding him . . . watching over him . . . Malachim . . . Derech . . . Coming and Going. Now and Forever.

"Caleb, it is time," intoned his father haltingly and lovingly.

Caleb stepped out of the elevator backwards not wanting to turn his back on his father or grandfather. In these final moments, his grandfather gazed serenely and deeply at Caleb who with tears in his eyes softly smiled at his grandfather as the doors closed. Almost. A light was let out forever.

Now, Caleb is challenged like never before. Losing his grandfather at an old age albeit painful is a wound quickly embalmed in the comfort of his final visit and words intoned by his grandfather to him. It feels like a crescendo to the symphony of his life. His mom's tragic death is a searing cut to his heart, a symphony whose light went out too soon like Hayden's Farewell Symphony #45.

Not only does Caleb begin to question God more deeply but he begins to feel a deep sense of guilt.

His dad would remind Caleb often of the ancient teaching to wake up like a lion to serve the Creator. A new day, new purpose. Now the words ring hollow.

He has been taught that he should be conscious of God's presence even while lying in bed in the morning. He should be grateful that his soul has been restored to him, that he did not pass away during the night, and that he has an opportunity to serve God in the new day.

This is the consciousness Caleb should have, but what has his consciousness become instead? What had forced him to get on the subway and go to a center of depravity like Times Square? Maybe, as Elijah suggested, God had a plan for him to go to Times Square—to descend into that pit—as a necessary step in order to then rise above it. Sometimes things like that have to happen. The people of Israel had to endure bondage in Egypt in order for the Exodus to take place. Maybe that's what's happening.

But here's the worst possibility. Something truly terrifying. What if by going to Times Square and throwing his LSAT book in the trash had somehow caused his mother's sudden illness and even her death? Had Elijah somehow known that? Is that why he had ended their conversation so abruptly? Had he thought there was still some way that Caleb could have prevented the catastrophe?

But he's not able to confront that now. He has to get out of bed. He has to wash his hands. He has to put on tefillin and pray, and he has to do these things with a sense of rigorous commitment that's been weakening for a while.

Today through the closed door of his bedroom Caleb can hear Jessie in the kitchen. When Caleb had returned from work last night, Jessie's door had been closed and there had been no light shining under the door. Jessie must have gone to bed early after a weekend with his family in upstate New York.

In the kitchen Jessie gives Caleb an English muffin and offers sympathy about Elyse's passing. Jessie's visit to Caleb during shiva was very meaningful but they are both so busy, they had not spoken recently.

Jessie's father is an orthodox rabbi in upstate New York, an area with a mostly Italian-American demographic. It isn't like growing up in New York City. Caleb senses that Jessie's devotion to Judaism is mainly an expression of loyalty to his father, but they haven't discussed it. Instead, they share intense opinions of the New York sports teams. Jessie is a huge fan and sports is their most frequent topic of conversation.

This morning Caleb takes things in a different direction. "A weird thing happened just before my mom died," Caleb says. He's going to tell Jessie about Elijah. But should he talk about Times Square?

"What happened?"

"I met somebody in Midtown, a guy who works as a street sweeper."

"Like with a broom?" Jessie asks. "I didn't think anybody did that anymore."

"I didn't think so either. But that's not the weird part. His name is Elijah, and I think he's a holy man. He seemed to know a lot about me, and then all of a sudden he told me I had to leave, like he knew something important was happening. It was like he knew my mom was going to die."

Jessie is listening closely, but Caleb senses that he's skeptical. "Well, I know this is a hard time for you. You've been under a lot of pressure."

"I'm serious, Jessie. This guy is the real thing."

"But what did he actually say to you? What great teachings did he bestow upon you?"

It's an important question, and Caleb doesn't have an answer right away. "Maybe it wasn't anything like great teaching. But he seemed to know that I've been starting to question some things."

"But I know that too. We've talked about it."

That's true. Caleb has let Jessie know that he's having doubts about how to live his life. He certainly has doubts about being a lawyer, although that's Sam's fervent wish for him. When Elyse died, Caleb had been ready to blame God. Now he blames himself. He has to be more observant. Or maybe he has to start being really observant for the first time.

How can he explain this to Jessie, who's on a clear path toward becoming a certified public accountant? Jessie will be taking the state exam in a few months. How could Jessie, for whom life seems clear, see that Caleb's life is the opposite of clear?

"He had a book that explains everything. It's called *The Secret of the Light.*"

Jessie grins. "Wow. Where can I get a copy?"

Then he says something that shows how much he cares about his friend. "You ought to talk with Rabbi Katz."

Caleb hasn't thought at all about Rabbi Katz, who is the *mashgiach ruchani*, the spiritual advisor, at Yeshiva University. Rabbi Katz has been a powerful influence on the Yeshiva students, including Caleb while he had been there. It isn't only what Rabbi Katz says. It is what he is: a flawless model of what a man can be in the Modern Orthodox tradition. But for that very reason, he can seem intimidating. Caleb has never had a personal conversation with Rabbi Katz.

He says, "Jessie, that's a fantastic idea. How do you think I should contact him?"

Jessie shrugged. "After work just go to the *beit midrash* at Yeshiva. He's always there."

But Rabbi Katz will have to wait.

Like every day over the last couple of weeks, Caleb scoots out of work mid-afternoon, lost in his thoughts at a bar near work. Every day a familiar cast of lost souls sit, ties undone, sipping some beers, an occasional shot of scotch and lost in their own thoughts.

As he sits in the bar a block away from his law office, he hears a familiar voice.

"Caleb, do you hear me?"

Startled, Caleb looks up and answers with surprise at who he thinks he sees in front of him.

"Yes . . . I am here . . . ."

"I almost didn't recognize you."

Caleb has not shaved nor gotten a haircut since his mom's burial, a mark of his state of mourning.

"Elijah?"

"Yes. It has been a month since your mom passed away."

"How did you know? What are you doing here?"

"Actually, my dentist is near here."

Caleb does not know whether to believe Elijah. His first encounter with Elijah in Times Square had been mysterious and surreal and now to see him in midtown outside his law office. The last time he has seen Elijah was before his mom passed away.

"Caleb, I heard about your mom. I am truly sorry and can only imagine the grief. I actually did not know where to find you, but I do not believe our encounter is random. I was walking on the sidewalk but, as I always do, keeping an eye out for impact opportunities, and lo and behold, I found you."

"Caleb, can I take a seat for a few minutes?"

Caleb shakes his head as if to awaken himself from his slumber and pulls a chair back for Elijah. Wearing a baseball cap tightly pulled over his head and a Parker coat, orange peeking out from the inside and a fake fur hood decked on top of the dark blue exterior, Elijah does not look the part of a holy man. Yet, his eyes reflect ancient wisdom and a giving spirit.

"Caleb, ever think about your name?"

"Not really. What do you mean?"

"The meaning of your name."

Caleb responded, "I know that Caleb was one of the messengers sent by Moses along with eleven others to investigate the land of Israel. Tragically, ten of the leaders fomented fear amidst the Jewish people and only Caleb and Joshua exuded optimism and faith. "

"Exactly. Don't get me wrong. There were tremendous obstacles facing the Jewish people upon entering the land of Canaan but Caleb in particular possessed a renewed spirit and proclaimed, "We shall go up!" He truly believed that in any moment, his role was to instill hope in places of despair. You will learn more I believe soon but for now, listen carefully. It is the first step in living the secret of the light and a path forward for you."

Caleb shifts in his chair as if to draw closer to Elijah.

Elijah continues slowly, "We cannot choose what happens to us, Caleb, but we can choose how to respond. It is not easy for sure when the world seems so foreboding and dark, but we all have a choice. Do we lament the darkness or increase the light?"

Caleb raises his head hopefully to Elijah allowing the words to wash over him.

Caleb cannot fathom how and why Elijah finds him in the middle of Manhattan, one of the busiest and largest cities in the world but somehow he feels that it is as if his mom wants him to hear these words now and like an arrow hitting the bullseye from far away, Elijah's words penetrate his heart.

"Elijah, I do not know what to say. This entire month is such a blur to me. Intellectually, I know I have to break free, to somehow mourn my mom but also re-enter the world carrying her with me. It is hard to find strength."

"Caleb, your name reflects the essence of your calling in life. Rise up—Caleb's words from thousands of years ago are yours too. Your mom's passing leaves a vacuum in the world but the greatest tribute you can give her is to fill the world with her light, her values. God will give you the strength to rise where you never felt possible."

"Thank you, Elijah."

"Caleb, I have to run to my appointment. We will meet again. I know."

Elijah pushes his chair back. "God bless you, Caleb. It may seem at this moment that I am here for you, but you are also meant to be here for me."

Caleb does not understand Elijah's words but still feels comforted by them although he is not sure why.

As Elijah rises, he places his hand on Caleb's head and incants the ancient prayer: "May God send his angels to watch over you every step of your way." With that, Elijah turns away and exits the coffee shop leaving Caleb in his wake feeling a renewed sense of spirit and purpose.

The next morning seems like a fresh start for Caleb.

The office officially opens at nine but Caleb and Marvin, the other clerk, have to arrive by eight to turn on the lights, check the firm's voicemail, and make sure the coffee is made.

When Caleb arrives today just before eight Marvin is already there, which isn't unusual. Marvin loves the law as much as Caleb doesn't love it. Even the most routine work at the firm is exciting to him. Like Caleb, he's studying like mad for the LSAT but no prep course for Marvin. He's high energy and motivated all the time.

Marvin is interested in Caleb's Orthodox Judaism because he sees a connection with the law. What really fascinates Marvin is the complexity of orthodox practice and the legalistic minutiae of it. Religion is one of his favorite subjects. He's done a lot of reading.

Once, during a lunch break, Marvin had begun a profound discourse. "From what I've been able to learn," he had said, "there's some dispute over what it means to be 'the chosen people.' One idea is that God chose to give the Torah to the Jews because they were in some way the most deserving of it. But there are also stories that God offered it to everybody else and they all turned it down. The Jews were the only ones that were willing to take it on."

"That's true," Caleb said. "There are different interpretations."

"Because just think about it," Marvin continues. "There's that big moment in the book of Genesis when God says to Avraham, 'I want you to drop whatever you're doing and go to a place that I'll show you.' God doesn't say where that is, and he doesn't say why he picked Avraham. He just says, 'Go to a place that I'll show you and I'll make you the founder of a great nation.' Of course, he doesn't say when that will happen either. How many people would go for a proposition like that? Not many, right?"

"Well, there is a backstory," Caleb answered. "God came to Abraham at seventy-five years old, but Abraham began his journey decades earlier. He began to question the mores of his time, who really runs the world, and he chose God as much as God chose him."

"I never thought about it that way, Caleb." Marvin had been so excited about this, and his energy had been contagious. It had been inspiring to look at the traditional teachings from new angles.

But today, Marvin is subdued. Until now, Caleb has been distant since returning to the firm after his mother's death but now he can sense a change in Caleb's demeanor. He immediately stops what he's doing and greets Caleb with a hug.

He says, "I just want to let you know again how sorry I am about your mom. Let me know if there's any way I can help."

"Thanks, Marvin. It has been such a rough road. I hope I will find the strength to carry my mom with me wherever I go," Caleb reflects, thinking about his encounter with Elijah at the bar.

"Well, today may be a day for a reboot. You're going to be busy. Perhaps that will help as you will be immersed in the business of work. It is too painful to have too much time to dwell on your sadness. Butenhamer has given me a big project that I'm really excited about. The only thing is, it's going to take me away from the filing and stuff."

Lois Butenhamer, new to the firm, is the only female partner and she's eager to make her mark. "That's okay, I can handle it," Caleb said. "What's the project?"

Marvin immediately brightens, as he does when any legal topic is involved. "She's writing an article that's basically about how much responsibility for unintelligent people is legally assumed by any service provider. For example, if city buses have a notice at every seat warning people not to stick their heads out of the window, is the city still liable if some people do it anyway, because they're really dumb."

He pauses dramatically. "The courts seem to be saying that the answer is yes. What do you think is going to happen?"

"You won't be able to open the windows on buses."

"That's right! That's exactly right!" Marvin exclaims, excited by the whole thing.

Within an hour the empty office shifts into frantic activity. It stays that way until five o'clock and beyond and the intensity is always on a nonstop high. A misplaced comma can completely change the meaning of a contract, which can ignite horrified screaming in a partner's office. Most of Caleb's work is routine, but it still has to be completed and tracked in great detail.

Much of the firm's business is in patents and corporate law. The New York based firm has a nearly century-long reputation for providing the highest-quality legal work and client service. They serve clients in a wide range of practice areas, including corporate, litigation, real estate, insolvency and restructuring, tax planning and highly ranked intellectual property division.

Caleb's work takes place in the office itself. It involves filing, printing, and proofreading documents before they go to the secretaries to become final drafts. This is where the misplaced commas become so important. Concentration is important, which isn't always easy with angry, red-faced lawyers stalking around the office.

Another aspect of Caleb's work consists of whatever miscellaneous tasks the partners feel like assigning. This can mean going to the dry cleaner, making bank deposits, or making dinner reservations over the phone.

Sometimes, but rarely, a partner will recruit Caleb or Marvin for work on a special project. This is how Marvin starts doing the research for Lois Butenhamer. In the nine months he's been working at the firm, Caleb has never been given such an assignment.

Around ten o'clock that morning Julius Golter, a senior partner, takes Caleb aside as he's putting ink in a printer. Among the staff, partners are always referred to by their last names only. "I'm so sorry about your mom. I've known your dad and mom for a long time. Elyse was one in a million," Golter says.

Then he shifts gears. "Let's meet in my office at 11:30, okay?"

"Yes, sure."

"Great." Golter gives Caleb a pat on the shoulder and hurries away.

It's an exciting development, but it means a stressful morning for Caleb. Since Marvin will be working with Butenhamer, Caleb will have to finish all of his proofreading by late morning. To his credit, as is usually the case when faced with a deadline, he gets it done with a few minutes to spare.

Golter has a corner office with a view of the bustling midtown streets. The firm is on the seventeenth floor of the building, not the highest but good enough to seem "above it all."

Golter is friendly enough. As a senior partner, he has nothing to prove. Instead of stationing himself behind his desk as most of the partners tend to do, he and Caleb sit together on a sofa at the far end of the office.

Golter says, "I'm so sorry about your mother, Caleb. It's terrible, really shocking. If there's anything we can do, estate issues of any kind, just let me know and we'll take care of it. She was obviously a really wonderful person."

Golter concludes with a sad shake of his head. Caleb has heard lots of condolences, but this deeply moves him. As a rule, the law firm is strictly business. It's gratifying to hear a human note struck by a full partner in the firm. Maybe there is hope for him in law after all.

"Thank you so much," Caleb says.

Golter takes a deep breath and returns to the matter at hand. "You've been doing a good job for us and don't think we haven't noticed. You're seeing the nuts and bolts of everyday law, which is certainly important but not exactly the most exciting thing in the world. Let's talk about something more interesting."

"More interesting?"

"Sure. This will be a chance to learn something very important. Did it ever occur to you that behind everything you see in this room—or in any room for that matter, any restaurant, any doctor's office—behind everything you see, there's somebody who made a fortune on it?"

Caleb hesitated. "I'm not sure I understand."

"Well, take sliced bread, for example, or individually sliced pieces of cheese. Whoever came up with those innovations made a fortune, right?"

"Sure."

"The milking machine is the same thing. The machine that milks cows. Just imagine if you got money every time a dairy farm licenses your patent which is renewable every year. Even if it is just a dollar or so, that's a huge amount of money. Well, our client, Danvers Hobson, is the heir to the great milking machine fortune, except now the patent is about to expire so Danvers is getting nervous. But there's really nothing to worry about."

"We help with the patent?"

"That's right. As the expiration for the patent comes closer—we call that the patent cliff—Danvers needs to be calmed down. It's just a procedural matter to renew the patent, or there could even be a gigantic lump sum payment if there is a buyout of some sort. You see what I mean?"

"Yes, I think so," Caleb says.

"Great, because we need to show Danvers that we're taking this seriously, So I'd like you to please hand deliver some papers to his apartment and then maybe spend a little time with him. You'll meet his wife too, of course. Her name is Mouse."

Golter is obviously very serious about this. Caleb nods appropriately. Golter says, "They're an interesting older couple. They'll enjoy having someone like you to talk with."

"Should I go today?"

"No. We're going to put the paperwork in an envelope and then I'll arrange a good time for you to show up. It will be later this week."

The meeting is over. Golter shakes Caleb's hand. You'll enjoy meeting Danvers and Mouse."

Caleb heads back to his office. As he is having a cup of coffee, the phone on his desk rings.

That phone rarely rings and it's generally a bad sign when it does. Most often it's a partner calling from his office down the hall asking for an errand to the dry cleaner.

But not this time. Caleb picks up the phone.

"Caleb, it's your Uncle Maish."

"Hi Maish, is everything okay?"

"Sure, no problems at all."

"Okay. Good."

"This is really a big adjustment for all of us, Caleb. Sometimes people don't want to think about how things affect them. But it's important to be honest about your emotions. You have to adjust to the new situation."

Caleb wonders if Maish is reading from something he's

written out beforehand. Caleb says, "Maish, I am confronting my emotions. I'm adjusting to the situation."

"I know you are. But you know, it's not good for a man to be alone. That's what God says, right?"

"Yes."

"I was speaking to your dad last night. Your mom's passing is painful for all of us and your dad is certainly not thinking of remarrying. It is the farthest thing from his mind. But he has been thinking about you and your future."

Caleb listens a bit more intently on the phone.

"The verse in the Bible tells us that after Abraham lost his wife Sara, his focus was on finding a wife for his son Isaac. Movingly, once Isaac finds Rebekkah as a wife, he becomes comforted after the loss of his mother. I realize this seems quick, only a month after my sister died, but we are worried about you and want you to think about your beginning to try to find your soul mate, your life partner."

"Yeah, I appreciate the thought, Uncle Maish. Dad's always getting on me about that," Caleb says, wearily. "What am I supposed to do, put an ad in the newspaper? I'm already working in this law firm for him."

"Your dad wants me to talk to you about it. He thinks I know a lot of young Jewish women in the jewelry business."

But Caleb has had enough. "Okay, I'll give it some thought, Maish. I appreciate your concern. Thanks for calling. But I think we've both got work to do now."

Sleep isn't coming that night. In his darkened room, Caleb listens to the sounds of the city through a partly opened window. There are sirens as always, sometimes nearby on

Broadway or else faintly in the distance. Emergencies are happening to people always and everywhere. And he's one of those people now. That's how he feels. But what kind of emergency is he in?

His mother's death was certainly an emergency. He'll never forget being in that hospital room, the touch of her hand at the last moment. But those moments are already fading into the past, although he doesn't want that to happen. But if it seems to be happening by itself, is that his fault?

He turns on the lamp beside his bed. He thinks about Nora, he thinks about Sam, and he thinks about Maish. Should he call Maish about meeting a future wife? Maybe he should call him right now?

No, it's too late at night. Calling now would seem crazy. On the other hand, Maish is a little crazy himself.

He turns off the light. All at once the scale of what's happening rises up before him like an iceberg in the Atlantic. His mother's death. His job. His worrisome faith. Finding your soulmate, which truly is one of life's most important enterprises and maybe the most important one of all.

It's not like dating in the secular world. For one thing, there can be no physical contact before marriage. It is rooted in the concept that enduring love emerges not from physical attraction but a deeper connection of two souls. The first touch is reserved for marriage to enhance the electricity of the moment. Dating is an exploration of chemistry, friendship, values and of course attraction. Yet, within marriage, Judaism celebrates intimacy not only to bring children into the world but to reveal deep pleasure and love between a husband and wife.

Lying in the darkness with all these thoughts running

through his mind, Caleb wonders if he should pray now. But what would his prayer be?

He's sure he'll be awake all night. But he soon falls deeply asleep.

On the subway the next morning, Caleb is in a strange, contradictory state of mind. He still feels emotionally and physically worn out, but also exhilarated in an artificial way, as if he's taken an energy pill. There's just so much going on. For the first time in his life, he feels like he should write a to-do list in order to keep track of it all. Maybe he can do that as soon as he gets to work. He can use the notebook he keeps in his desk to track his court filings.

Arriving at the firm, Caleb finds a post-it note from Golter on the desk he shares with Marvin. "Please see me immediately."

Marvin, who has arrived early as usual, glances at Caleb with raised eyebrows. "Golter must have put this here after you left yesterday. What do you think it's about?"

"Let's talk about it later," Caleb says, and he walks quickly out of the office.

Although it's not yet eight o'clock, the firm is beginning a new workday. Associates—non-partner lawyers, many only recently out of law school—are expected to work twelve-hour days, plus weekends, so they're already busy in their windowless offices, like bees in a hive serving the Queen. The associates try to outdo each other. Some of them almost live at the firm, sleeping on the floor several nights each week. In return for this, even new associates are paid an amazing amount of money. That can end quickly, or it can multiply if they make partner. Not surprisingly, in large law firms, divorce is not uncommon. Attorneys spend more time and energy on their law firm relationship than their relationship with their spouse. It is not an easy road to navigate.

In his large office, Golter is in a good mood when Caleb arrives. "Great news! They want to meet you today!"

"The Hobson couple?"

Golter comes from behind his desk holding a big manila envelope. "Here's the patent paperwork. They're early risers, so get over there by nine o'clock. Take a cab. Charge it to the firm," Golter declares, with a sweeping gesture of his arm.

He scrawls an address on the envelope and hands it to Caleb. "Caleb, these people are important clients so remember that you're representing the firm. Just keep a smile on your face. Act interested. Laugh at their jokes."

"Absolutely," Caleb agrees.

"Excellent. Check in with me when you get back."

The address on the envelope is One Beekman Place. Caleb has no idea where that might be, but he expects it to be very high end, and it is. In fact, One Beekman Place is a famously classy address in Manhattan, a sixteen-story pre-war apartment building just north of the United Nations on the East River.

Under a green canopy supported by highly polished brass poles, Caleb presents himself to the young doorman at One Beekman Place. "I'm visiting the Hobson family from the law firm Shultz and Golter. "

"I'll let them know you're here," the doorman says. He punches a single-digit number on a wall phone beside the door. After a few words are exchanged, the doorman hangs up the phone. "Twelfth floor," he says, holding the door open for Caleb.

Next stop is the elevator with its human operator, something almost unheard of in late-twentieth century Manhattan. They cruise up to the twelfth floor. There are only two apartments. The silent operator, an older man, helpfully points to one of the doors, then starts his descent.

Caleb is alone in the small hallway, standing before the correct door. To his left is a narrow table, and somehow he automatically understands that each day the elevator operator places the day's mail for the occupants of these two apartments on that table. How does he know that? It just seems so right.

Now, should he knock on the door or press the doorbell on the jamb? He presses the doorbell. Three musical notes are heard, gentle and ascending.

Caleb waits. He takes a deep breath. He's feeling apprehensive although the envelope from the firm is a reassuring prop, like a passport. A long moment passes. Should he ring again? That might be risky.

The door opens and a woman slightly taller than Caleb smiles and says, "Hello, hello, we're expecting you, please come in." She's wearing faded blue jeans, a kind of smock, also blue but a darker shade than her jeans, buttoned up to her neck. Her iron-gray hair hangs loose over her shoulder like a folk singer's. She looks like a recently retired athlete, maybe an Olympic diver. It's hard to imagine that her name is Mouse, but as she steps aside for Caleb to enter she says, "How are you today? My name is Mouse."

"I'm Caleb." He smiles and briefly grasps her offered hand.

"Let me get Danvers. We have a vizsla, and every morning Danvers spends an hour putting her through her paces. Do you have a dog?"

"No, I don't," Caleb admits. "I do like them though."

"Danvers, the young man from Shultz is here!" Mouse shouts.

Her voice is loud and strong. Suddenly Caleb understands, in the same way he understood about the mail delivery, that Mouse is called Mouse because she's so unlike a Mouse. Like a tall person named Shorty.

"Coming, coming . . ."

That's a man's voice, coming from somewhere deep in the apartment, which Caleb already knows is an apartment unlike any he's seen before. It's not what he would have expected in a staid building on Beekman Place. Even here in the entrance hall—the foyer, whatever it's called—the walls are hung with framed drawings whose subjects he can't make out. But he knows they're all extremely valuable. Once again, somehow he just knows that.

Mouse sighs. "There's no stopping Danvers once he gets started with Olivia. Come on, we'll distract him from his dog."

She keeps talking as Caleb follows her through a maze of rooms furnished from various historical eras and worldwide locations. Each room is decorated with a bewildering variety of paintings, sculptures, and framed drawings, etchings, and even some black and white photographs.

"Do you like art?" Mouse is saying. "Collecting is what we live for. There was a married couple that lived on the Upper West Side. They weren't especially wealthy; I believe the gentleman worked in the post office. They started collecting unknown artists early in their marriage and they just kept it up. After a while the artists weren't unknown anymore, far from it, and they used to give their works to this couple who had supported them at the beginning. All the while the couple was living in the same one-bedroom apartment. Eventually the apartment was totally filled with art, literally every inch. They couldn't even use the oven in the kitchen because there was a painting in there. So they sold their collection to a major museum. Three moving trucks came to get everything. They got millions of dollars, of course."

"That's an amazing story," Caleb says. "He probably didn't have to work at the post office anymore."

"I believe he had retired from the post office by the time they sold their collection. The point is, if they could pack that much stuff into a one-bedroom apartment, imagine what we can do with a big place like this. We're working on it."

They're in a room distinguished by a gracefully curving staircase. As Caleb realizes that the apartment occupies two floors, a sleek russet-colored dog comes bounding down the stairs followed by a shoeless man in a blue silk bathrobe. He is tall and lean, a bit taller than Mouse, and he wears a look of good-natured exasperation as the dog jumps on Caleb. This is Danvers.

"Olivia, will you please control yourself!" he commands, but it's useless. The dog is excited to greet a newcomer.

"Don't mind Olivia," Danvers says. "She's just two years old. I'm glad to see you're a dog lover. Vizslas, as you may know, are bundles of energy and Olivia is especially energetic in the morning. We've been running around since five-thirty and normally she would be getting ready for a nap about now but of course that's out of the question now. Anyway, you're here from the law firm? I'm Danvers. Pleased to meet you."

"Hi, I'm Caleb." They shake hands as Mouse distracts Olivia.

"Would you like something to eat?" Mouse asks. "Some coffee or tea? Olivia is going to eat. Let's go into the kitchen."

At a marble counter in the bright and sunny kitchen a young woman is opening a can of dog food. "Anna, meet Caleb. Caleb, meet Anna," Danvers says.

Anna looks up. "Hi," she says.

"Hi, Anna."

Caleb is still holding the manila envelope. So far no one has shown any interest in it. This seems to be turning into a purely social visit.

"Let's sit over here," Mouse suggests, heading for a breakfast table under a window. "Coffee is already made, but we can make some fresh if you're a real coffee person. We have tea also, of course."

"Orange juice too," Danvers says, as he removes a pitcher from the refrigerator. "I just squeezed it this morning." He places the pitcher on the table, then returns with three glasses and sits down.

"Anna is from Hungary," Mouse says, as she pours juice. "Vizslas are Hungarian dogs so we thought they might respond well to each other, and they really do."

Danvers says, "Most people don't have the luxury of giving their dog the best possible care. Most people aren't able to collect art like we do either. My grandfather happened to be a genius who invented and patented the first mechanical milking machine. We lease those machines all over the world and receive money every time our patent is licensed. It is renewable annually. That's why we have these luxuries."

Caleb says, "Wow. By the way, this is for you from Mr. Golter." He passes the envelope to Danvers.

"Is it something urgent?"

"I really don't know anything about it."

"It's nothing urgent. Patent renewal. The firm wants to show that they're earning their fees from us."

Mouse says, "Are you orthodox, Caleb? Because I notice you're wearing a skullcap."

Caleb sees that she's asking this with the utmost sincerity, as if his obvious Jewishness is the most fascinating thing in the world.

"I'm modern orthodox," he says.

"But what does modern orthodox really mean?"

"Well, modern orthodox Judaism means engagement with the contemporary world together with a life of religious observance. It's different from the Hasidic practice we see in Crown Heights or Williamsburg. Basically, the Hasidic rabbis came to America after the war and created communities that tried to duplicate Jewish life as it existed in Europe. But modern orthodox means integrating with the surrounding world rather than isolating from it. Also, unlike many of the Hasidim, modern orthodoxy affirms the spiritual value of the state of Israel."

"That's very interesting," Mouse says, again with a disarming sincerity. "There are wonderful artists in Israel. We have a nice Ychoshua Gips charcoal drawing."

"Yehoshua Gips?"

"Yes. Do you know his work?"

"I've heard his name." Caleb belies his connection.

"Would you like to see the drawing? It's upstairs."

"I'd love to. But I really should get back to the firm."

"Well, you can see it next time then. Finish your orange juice."

The rest of the day passes without incident. Golter seems satisfied with Caleb's report about the Hobsons, although he wishes they had been more interested in the manila envelope. Big clients are wooed by other firms. There is always a chance of a client bolting.

That isn't Caleb's concern. With Marvin preoccupied elsewhere, Caleb files some papers and leaves for home.

So much going on, everything pulling him in different directions. He feels like he isn't handling things very well. If only he could talk to his mom. Of course, he actually can talk to her. But can she talk back to him?

It's not good for a man to be alone. Sam and Maish are again starting up about him meeting a woman. The worst part is, there's truth in it.

Jessie's suggestion about reaching out to Rabbi Katz at the *beit midrash* is a good idea. Walking toward the subway station after work, Caleb sees no reason why he can't go to the *beit midrash* right now. There's no need to even go home first. Rabbi Katz is a wise man. He will certainly listen closely to Caleb's concerns.

By the time he boards the "A" train at 59th Street, Caleb has made up his mind. He is going to see Rabbi Katz.

But something happens that surprises Caleb himself. He gets off the train at 72nd Street and heads back downtown.

The person he wants to see is not Rabbi Katz, despite his great respect for that eminent man. The person he wants to see is Elijah. He wants to go to Times Square.

On the train heading south, he feels an immediate sense of relief. He also feels confident. Elijah has a presence that goes beyond the wisdom that Caleb has found even in his best teachers. It is amazing how Elijah seemed to know that Caleb should leave immediately. Somehow Elijah knew that Elyse was close to death. Elijah appeared again as he sat in the coffee shop in a fog a month after his mother's death. It isn't just wisdom. It is a prophecy. A prophet is someone who can talk with God and lives in the slipstream of Godliness.

As he emerges from Port Authority on 42nd Street, Caleb feels the exhilaration of being in Times Square. Going there is a transgression and transgression is exciting. Perhaps the struggle with his faith leads him towards the lights of Times Square. It's like watching the kind of movie he had never been allowed to watch, but sometimes he had watched anyway. Now he's a character in the movie, but he can step out of the movie whenever he wants. He can just get back on the "A" train.

On 43rd Street he approaches the door where he and Elijah had met for the first time. He can hardly remember when that meeting took place. Things seem to happen all at once since Elyse's death, but everything also seems to move farther back into the distant past.

The door with the Star of David is still where he expects it to be. Had Elijah unlocked the door on his previous visit? Or was the door unlocked, open to all comers, which would be very tzaddik-like?

Even if the door is unlocked Caleb doesn't think he

should just walk in. He knocks, but the sound seems so weak against the door. He pushes against the door, and it opens.

Caleb finds himself in murky darkness. A candle is burning on the table where he had sat the other time. That's the only light.

"Hello?" he says. "Elijah?"

"Oh, hi . . ."

A woman is walking toward him. She's the most beautiful woman he's ever seen and irresistible.

What's she doing here? What's he doing here?

"How can I help you, sir?" she says in a serious tone. Or is it sarcastic?

"I'm looking for Elijah. We met the other day."

"That's so wonderful. I mean, it's wonderful that you met him, and it's wonderful that you want to meet him again. But he's not here right now, unfortunately."

Somehow Caleb feels like he's seen her before. Maybe he's seen her on the subway. She's wearing a soft white sweater, possibly cashmere, and a dark skirt. He looks at her shoes. It seems odd that she's wearing running shoes, but he's noticed at the law firm that there are secretaries, paralegals, and even female partners who wear running shoes which they change for regular shoes upon arrival and then switch back to running shoes when they leave. But none of the men wear running shoes except Marvin. He always wears them.

"Would you like to sit down? Elijah will be back eventually."

She starts toward the table. When Caleb hesitates, she looks at him with concern.

"You're afraid of violating the rule against being alone with a woman, aren't you? Well, don't worry about it. Take a chance. Live dangerously. Roll the dice. All those rules and regulations are meant to be broken anyway. Everybody breaks them and then God makes you feel guilty about it. He knew Adam and Eve were going to eat the forbidden fruit. Of course he knew! Are you kidding me? It was all a setup! Einstein said God is devious but not malicious except I wouldn't be too sure about that. Oh well, sorry for the rant. Come and sit with me at the table. No one is watching us here, not even God. He never comes to Times Square."

They sit at the table. Caleb can see her better in the candlelight. I like talking to people," she continues. "But now it's your turn."

"Okay."

"My name's Orly. And you are . . . ?"

"Caleb."

" Caleb, who's your favorite biblical character?"

"I'm not sure I've ever thought about it that way," Caleb says. "Maybe Moses . . . ."

"Yes, Moses is a good one. He made some mistakes but who doesn't? My favorite character is the talking serpent."

"The talking serpent in the Garden?"

"Yes. Is there another talking serpent? Eve says that God told her they would die if they ate the fruit. But the serpent says they won't die, and they don't."

"Well, they do die eventually."

Orly shakes her head impatiently. "But he didn't say anything. He said today. He said, 'On the day that you eat thereof, you shall surely die.' That's a direct quote from God."

She laughs. Caleb isn't sure how to respond. Is she trying to be funny?

"Let me help you out, Caleb, because I know you're

63

interested in these spiritual matters. Here's what the serpent does. He—or is it she?—says this is the way things seem. The serpent says this is what you've been told. But I'm going to tell you the way things really are, and I'm also going to show you how to change the way things are."

She's staring directly at Caleb. "Do you want to change the way things are? You seem a little shy. Are you a shy person?"

"Well, I've been under a lot of stress. That's what I want to talk with Elijah about."

"Feeling stressed? Poor baby. What are you stressed about?"

"My mother died very recently. It was sudden."

"Oh, I'm sorry to hear that. But here's what you're really stressed about. You're frightened that the whole God thing is a big scam. Your mom's sudden death raised that possibility in your mind. How could something like that happen? Why did it happen? Did God make a bet with somebody, like in the Book of Job?"

She takes a book from the stack to her left. "See this?" she says, holding the book with both hands. "*The Secret of the Light.*"

"Can I see it?" Caleb asks, but she suddenly draws the book back toward her.

"It's time for you to go now," she says.

"Why do I have to go all of a sudden? That's what happened with Elijah."

"What a coincidence. But it's time for you to go."

"All right, but . . . will I see you again?"

"I'm sure you will."

"Where will I see you? When?"

"Oh, you're interested in me? I'm flattered. You have to go now, but there's something important I want you to do."

"What is it?"

"Well, when we were talking about the serpent, Eve told the serpent that God didn't want them to touch the tree. But actually God didn't say anything about touching the tree. That was all in her head. They could have touched it all they wanted as far as God was concerned."

"So what do you want me to do?"

Orly stands up. She holds her right hand in front of Caleb.

"Just touch my hand."

Caleb hesitates.

"Caleb, are you okay? What's going on, man?"

Caleb opens his eyes, blinking a couple of times. He's still in the fabric chair, but now Elijah is in front of him with a hand on his shoulder.

"What are you doing here, Caleb? Do you need help?"

Caleb manages a weak smile. "Maybe I do need help."

He glances around the room. "I thought we could talk for a while, so I came down to see you. There was someone else here though. A woman. Is she still here?"

Elijah looks shocked, like this is the craziest thing he's ever heard. "There's nobody here, Caleb." He sits down in the other chair. "I think you've got a lot on your mind, maybe too much. I want to help you if I can, but what you really need is rest. Some time off. Is that possible?"

Caleb gives Elijah a worried look. "Elijah, there was a woman here and I talked with her for a while. She said her name was Orly. Do you know anybody by that name?"

"Orly? That's a name you hear in Israel."

"Maybe she is from Israel."

"Well, you really need to get some rest. You can stay here if you want. Maybe take tomorrow off from work?"

Caleb gets to his feet. "I can't take tomorrow off." He turns toward the door. "But I'll be back."

As he is about to leave, Elijah motions to Caleb to wait. Caleb stops at the threshold of the door. Between two worlds.

"I cannot tell you if you imagined Orly or not. I can tell you that in order to grow, you must be tested. It is a principle of the secret of the light. Every descent, every temptation is a manifestation of God's desire to realize new potential in yourself and release new light in the world. I must go." To Caleb's surprise, Elijah turns away and opens a door behind him that Caleb had not even noticed existed.

PART TWO

A few weeks pass. Caleb remembers Elijah's words at the
bar. He is trying to focus on increasing the light, but the
encounters with Elijah and Orly leave him perplexed.

He tries to focus on the upcoming law school test. He
attends the final prep. He doesn't tell Sam about the class
that he missed.

The official test date is on a Saturday but for test-
takers who observe shabbat there's an alternative session
the following day. In a classroom at Columbia University,
with a dozen other Orthodox law school aspirants, the test's
perplexing questions occupy Caleb's attention at least for a
while.

> *A film festival at a university will screen three*
> *films*—Hope, Waste, *and* Curiosity. *The festival*
> *will be held on Thursday, Friday, and Saturday.*
> *Each film is shown at least once during the festival*
> *but never more than once on any day. On each day*
> *at least one film is shown. Films are shown one at a*
> *time.*
>
> *The following conditions apply: On Thursday*
> Waste *is shown, and no film is shown after* Waste
> *that day. On Friday either* Hope *or* Curiosity, *but*

*not both, is shown, and no other film is shown on
that day.*

On Saturday either Hope *or* Waste, *but not
both, is shown, and no other film is shown after it
on that day.*

> *Which one of the following CANNOT be true?*
> *(A)* Waste *is the last film shown each day of the
>   festival.*
> *(B)* Curiosity *is shown on each day of the
>   festival.*
> *(C)* Hope *is shown second on each day of the
>   festival.*
> *(D) A different film is shown first on each day
>   of the festival.*
> *(E) A different film is shown last on each day of
>   the festival.*

What interests Caleb, and also distracts him from
actually answering the question, are the titles of the three
Imaginary films: *Hope, Curiosity,* and *Waste.* What could
those movies possibly be like? Caleb wants to see those films
although he knows they don't exist and probably never could
exist. They were just random words selected by whatever
graduate student was getting paid to make up the test.

But the titles get him thinking. What is he hoping for?
What is he curious about? And most importantly, what is
being wasted in his life?

Certainly the time he's spending on this test is a
total waste. He's doing it to please Sam, pure and simple.
Whenever Caleb speaks to his father, Sam never fails to bring
up the LSAT. Where will the test be administered? How long

will the test take? Will Caleb be allowed to bring food into the room? Talking with Sam about the test is like taking a test in itself.

Maybe Orly is just a symptom of the stress he's been under for a long time, and especially since Elyse's death. He often thinks about Orly. In fact, he thinks about her all the time. He thinks he sees her during the day, usually on the subway. Maybe he should buy a pocket notebook to keep track of the sightings.

Caleb looks at his watch. He's been taking the test for almost an hour. The room is a lecture hall with rows of small desks accessible by a steeply sloping stairway. Looking around for a moment, he can almost feel an electric charge of concentration. Every desk is filled. There must be at least a hundred aspiring lawyers here, even on the alternate test day.

Maybe Orly is here. Could it be possible that Orly is taking the LSAT?

That is possible, but it's unlikely. There is no reason to believe this could happen. Still, Caleb scans the room.

Then he hears a sharp whisper.

"Sir . . ."

He looks to his left and sees the exam proctor staring straight at him. It's obviously another grad student like the ones who had made up the test in the first place. The guy doesn't look happy.

Caleb gives him a quizzical look, as if to say, "Who, me?"

"You need to keep your eyes on your paper."

As Caleb nods meekly in reply, at least half of all the test takers look around to see what the commotion is about. It's embarrassing. He makes an effort to look at his exam. He still hasn't completed the question about the three movies at the film festival. Even so, he skips ahead to the next question. It seems to be about a cruise ship that visits seven different ports.

But Caleb has had it. He's hit bottom with the law school stuff. For a moment his conversation with Golter had him feeling a bit hopeful about law, but that feeling has passed. He'll have to be honest about it with Sam. Leaving the incomplete test on his desk, he heads toward the door. Winding down after the test, Caleb isn't sure how to spend the rest of the afternoon. Nora is with Lily at Amanda and Glenn's apartment, and thank God for them. Caleb definitely needs to spend time with Nora tonight. Right now he could go back to his apartment on Bennett Avenue where Jessie is sure to be watching a baseball game or—and here's a good idea—he could go see Rabbi Katz.

Rabbi Katz! Just the thought of a man who's totally devoted to Torah study is reassuring to Caleb. Otherwise, he feels trapped in his own head by thoughts of his mom.

Psychologically, it's becoming complicated. If he stops thinking about his mom, if he stops mourning her, he feels like he's abandoning her. But he can never abandon her. He can never turn away from her.

He gets on an uptown train at 110th Street. He's on his way to see Rabbi Katz. In a literal translation, beit midrash means house of learning. At Yeshiva University, as in synagogues around the world, the *beit midrash* is a twenty-four-hour library and study hall. But for Rabbi Katz it's obviously much more, and everyone knows that.

He never seems to leave the *beit midrash*. He doesn't stop studying unless a student comes to him with a question. But if a student does approach him Rabbi Katz never resents the interruption. He always looks up from his book with a gentle smile, as if he'd actually been waiting for the student to appear.

From the 181st subway station it's a ten-minute walk to Yeshiva University. It's a walk Caleb has made hundreds of times when he was an undergraduate. As he makes the same walk now, he feels like he could be heading to class again. In fact, he wishes he were heading back to class. He used to dislike the idea that his daily schedule was all planned out for him, that someone was telling him what to do. But someone telling him what to do is exactly what he's looking for now.

It's mid-afternoon when Caleb arrives at the *beit midrash*, the large room with bookshelves filled with hundreds of books on Jewish topics. It's late Sunday afternoon. A few students are in the study hall preparing for the coming week.

At a table by himself Rabbi Katz sits with an open book before him. He holds an official appointment as spiritual advisor to the Yeshiva University community. He spends a lot of time in the study hall counseling the students.

As Caleb approaches the table, Rabbi Katz closes the book in front of him.

He skips any formal greeting. He says, "You've already graduated, haven't you?"

"Yes, I have."

"I remember seeing you here occasionally. Your name is . . ."

"Caleb."

"Yes. Caleb. Please sit down. How can I help you, Caleb?"

For the next five minutes Caleb tries to explain his state

of mind and heart. The death of his mother, his wavering interest in Jewish observance and spirituality, his work at the law firm to please his father, and how he generally feels adrift. He mentions Elijah and his surprise at finding such a man in Times Square. He does not mention Orly.

When he's finished speaking, Rabbi Katz leans toward him with an earnest look. "What is your mother's name?"

"Her name was Elyse."

"Caleb," Rabbi Katz says, "Not what *was* her name but what *is* her name?"

"Elyse."

"Where is Elyse buried?"

"In Israel. In Safed."

"Safed is a very holy city. It is the home of many great mystics past and present. Your mother's burial there is a testament to her spiritual depth."

Caleb nods his head as he listens intently.

With no hesitation Rabbi Katz continues, "I want to tell you about a sign I saw in Safed many years ago. *Guard the Silence*. The old quarter of Safed is one of the quietest cities. I never understood why until recently. I know you are having questions of faith. It is no coincidence that silence is so valued in Safed. Sometimes it is only in the silence, when we turn off all of the outside noise, that we can hear the Divine voice inside of us."

"Caleb, your mother never died. She is eternal."

"Rabbi, how do I feel her presence? Where do I find the faith?"

Rabbi Katz whispers, "Caleb, God is not in the thunder or lightning or the roar but in the still small voice we hear every day. It is inside of us and in the world around us."

"How do I hear it?" Caleb finally seems at a bit more peace.

"There's a book called *The Secret of the Light*. Do you know about that book?"

"I've heard of it. I've even seen it. But I don't know what's in it."

"Everything is in it."

"Everything?"

The rabbi nods affirmatively.

"Thank you for coming to see me, Caleb. I wish you the best. *Zei gezunt*. Be well."

The meeting has come to an abrupt end. Rabbi Katz sits down again and returns his attention to *Emanations from the Left Side*.

Traveling back to the 107th Street apartment, Caleb feels disappointed in his meeting with Rabbi Katz. He's disappointed in himself. He didn't say anything about his fascination with Times Square, about Elijah, or about Orly. Yet that's what's really on his mind. If he had brought them up, maybe Rabbi Katz would have had some practical advice. Instead, there were Torah stories. Not that Torah stories aren't great, but they aren't what he needs right now.

One thing he needs is a few quiet moments by himself. Since Nora is just down the hall with Lily, Caleb lets himself into Sam's apartment and lies down on the big green sofa in the living room. So many days, so many years he spent on this sofa, with the television set perfectly positioned across the room, and now here he is again. If he closes his eyes, he can hear his mother in the kitchen down the hall. What's for dinner tonight?

The telephone rings. Caleb knows he'd better answer

the phone. It might be Sam. He gets up and answers the phone. It is Sam.

"Hi, dad. Is anything wrong?"

"No, I just wanted to check in. Why should anything be wrong?

"Well, I just feel like this is kind of a sensitive time."

"No, no, everything's fine," Sam says. "Have you spoken to Maish about meeting any girls?"

Caleb has to stop himself from laughing at how quickly Sam brings this up. His father is becoming a matchmaker.

"Not yet, dad. But I will."

"And how's work going?"

"It's going well. A little more interesting. I met some clients who are art collectors. They even have some stuff by the artist you met when you were in Tzfat."

"Yehoshua Gips?"

"Yes."

There's a brief silence on the line. Then Sam comes back and he's extremely excited. Breathless.

"Caleb, that's fantastic. This is an amazing coincidence. I've stayed in touch with Yehoshua Gips. I was going to tell you about it, but I didn't think you'd be interested."

"So what's the big coincidence?"

Now Sam sounds impatient. "Caleb, Yehoshua Gips is finishing a painting of the letter *aleph*, the silent letter. But it's not always silent, and there may even have been a time when it wasn't silent at all. Anyway, he feels this is a very important work. The most important painting he's ever done."

"That's great, Dad. But so what?"

"So what? So what?" Sam repeats. "Here's so what,

Caleb. Yehoshua Gips is sick and tired of the gallery system. He wants to find somebody for a private sale of his *aleph* painting. Do you see the connection now?"

"I've met some art collectors. Is that the connection?"

"That's right. I assume they're extremely wealthy?"

"Yes. They get money annually every time a dairy farm licenses their patent."

Sam ignores this point of information. He says, "All right, you tell the art collectors how they can get in on the ground floor with this painting. Yehoshua Gips has explicitly told me that he's looking for a private buyer, and he also told me that whoever can find a buyer for him gets a commission. See what I mean?"

"Yes, I see."

"You don't sound very enthusiastic."

"I'll mention it to them."

"I'm trying to help you out."

"I understand, dad. I'll mention it to them."

Another silence. Then, "How's Nora?"

"She seems good. She's with Lily. I'm going to get her now."

"Okay. Don't forget what we've talked about."

"I'll never forget it. Really, never."

Nora is beside Caleb on the green sofa. She's tired after a day with Lily, but Caleb has been looking through Sam's cache of family letters and Caleb wants Nora to know about them. He shuffles through them quickly and randomly picks one from his mom.

He reads:

Dear Caleb,
Thank God, I am feeling much better after having a
terrible cold over the holiday. How was your Sukkot
traveling around Israel? What did you do for the last
day of the holiday? I am sure by the time you receive
this letter, I will have received one from you but
sometimes the time lag between letters is frustrating.

Did you ever receive the Sports Illustrated *I*
mailed you?

Dad has looked into flights to visit you in
Israel. Now that we are buying a new car I'm not
sure we have the money for both of us to come so we
will keep you informed.

Learn well. We love you and miss you,
Mom

Reading this aloud, Caleb is literally moved beyond
words. The emotion mingled with everyday details is what
makes it so powerful.

"That's from when I was spending a year in Israel," he says.

"Yeah." Nora looks at him blankly.

"Here's another one"

Dear Caleb,
We just got off the phone with you. We love you and
miss you so much! It's expensive to call Israel but so
very wonderful to speak with you.

Today was a special breakfast at the school.
Jason and his committee did a wonderful job. They
served cereal, milk, bagels, cream cheese and juice
and Rabbi Tolner gave a Torah insight. I enjoyed my

*weekend at the Goldbergs for the Bat Mitzvah. Now
I have to get back into the swing of things at home
and at school. I teach 6 hours and tutor during
lunch and sometimes at the end of school. I hardly
have time to make up and mark quizzes. I enjoy
working but find it very demanding.*

It's late now. Learn well and write soon!
Love,
Mom

"That's when she was a teacher, which she was for a long time. You can see how important my schoolwork was to her, like when she says, '"Learn well."'"

"Yeah."

Why has he decided to look at these letters with her? Now he feels like he's going to cry. He knows Nora sees this. It scares her. But he wants to do at least one more. Maybe an upbeat one. He shuffles through the letters.

"Here's one from me that I wrote from Israel . . ."

*I'm not exactly sure where to start but I want to
say Happy Birthday! I miss you and your "out of
this world" meals, and I miss even when you tell
me when I'm doing wrong. I don't really have that
happen in Israel which makes it much more of a
challenge for me. I'm doing my best to make the most
out of my time here. Thank you for all you do for
me! I love you very much!*

Wishing you the happiest of birthdays!
Love,
Caleb

"Do you see what I'm trying to say there?" Caleb turns to Nora.

"You're saying that you love her."

Suddenly, this is an astonishing moment for Caleb. For the first time, he sees how Sam feels. He sees how Nora just can't understand what he's trying to say to her, or what he wants her to say to him. Or maybe she understands all too well, and she is just not able to do that yet. Especially not now. Maybe someday, surely someday, but not now.

"I'm so tired," she says. "I'm really beat."

"Sleep well, Nora. Love you."

The next day around mid-morning, Golter calls Caleb into his office and says, "The Hobson couple were very impressed by you. I can't understand why."

This is supposed to be funny. To show he gets the joke, Caleb says, "Yeah, I really had them fooled."

"If they ever decide to liquidate the art collection or something let me know and we'll handle the legalities."

"I understand. What's the next step."

"Your job is just listening to them. I'll let you know about the next meeting. You won't have to do much."

"I'll just be a breath of fresh air."

"A ray of sunshine."

That afternoon Caleb files some papers in the office and then decides to call Maish. He owes that much to Sam.

Maish says, "I'm glad you called. I've got a gal for you."

"A gal?'

"Are you ready to meet her?"

"Can we talk about this for a minute?"

Maish's voice rises. "What is there to talk about? I've gone out of my way for you. I've talked to a lot of people about my nephew, the graduate of Yeshiva University, the impressive young man whose mother has just passed on and he's looking for a wife. What are you waiting for?"

"Well, can you give me her phone number?" He doesn't want to argue with Maish, who's well-known for flying off the handle.

"Listen, Caleb, I don't want you to embarrass me in front of this girl if you're not interested." Maish sounds even angrier than before.

"I can't embarrass you if you don't give me her phone number. I can't do anything, actually."

"She works for the William H. Glass Company. Pretty big wholesalers. Felix told me about her."

"Do you have her number, Uncle Maish?"

"I've got it here somewhere."

An uncomfortable silence follows. Caleb imagines Maish urgently searching his desk, his wallet, his wastebaskets.

Then: "What's the number where you're at? I'm going to call Felix. I'll call you right back."

"Okay, Uncle Maish."

Caleb gives Maish his direct line. As he is waiting for Maish to return the call, he sees a cop walking with one of the attorneys down the hall. Who is leading whom is not clear. Caleb wonders if he should become a police officer. Would that satisfy Sam? It's not that different from being a lawyer.

The phone rings. "All right, I called Felix and he put her on the line. I talked to her. She can meet you at seven tonight in the lobby of the Hotel Giraffe."

"The Hotel Giraffe? I've never heard of it. Do you know where that is?"

"I have no idea where it is!" Maish snaps. "Do I have to do everything for you? She'll meet you at seven o'clock at the Hotel Giraffe."

"I thought I was going to call her."

"We're skipping that part."

"Okay, I'll figure it out," Caleb says. He tries to sound enthusiastic. "Thanks, Maish. I'll be there."

"Don't embarrass me."

"I won't. What's her name?"

"Her name is Orly. She says it means light in Hebrew."

Oh my God, oh my God. Caleb cannot believe the coincidence. He realizes that he has to pop out of work to pick up some clothes from the dry cleaner for the evening. Hailing a cab, which is never easy but now seems impossible, as he emerges from the building onto the street. How can he do something like hail a cab?

But as he stands on the curb and raises his hand, an empty cab immediately pulls up. It's an amazing miracle, like the parting of the Red Sea. Caleb realizes that some fundamental change in the nature of reality must have just happened. Miracles are happening all the time now. He easily gets a cab, which proves it.

Furthermore, despite the usual midtown traffic, the driver is an aggressive type who gets him back to the office in minutes. As he pays the fare, Caleb asks, "Do you happen to know the location of the Hotel Giraffe?"

"The Hotel Giraffe," the driver repeats, and he needs to think for only a second. "Park Avenue South and 26th Street."

Another miracle. "Thank you, sir." Caleb gives him a big tip. He jumps out of the cab. His heart is pounding. Everything has changed.

Caleb makes it back to the firm within the hour and finds one of Golter's "see me" notes on his desk. As he hurries down the hall, a meeting is just breaking up in a partner's office. One of the attendees, obviously from another firm, looks like he's ready to explode as he narrowly avoids a collision with Caleb. His face is bright red. Veins are pulsing in his temples.

What could possibly bring a man to that point, Caleb wonders. A real estate deal? A personal injury case? Whatever it is, he can't imagine getting that agitated over any legal issue. Of course, he himself is also extremely agitated. But he has a good reason. It's about meeting Orly at the Hotel Giraffe.

Meanwhile he's still grappling with his relationship with God about what happened to his mom. He has to keep this in the forefront of his mind because anything else would be disrespectful of his mom's memory. So he's jumping out of his skin about meeting Orly while he's still angry at God.

Golter is on the phone when Caleb enters his office. He immediately ends the call.

"Hey, where have you been?" He says it with a smile, or a half-smile.

"I had to run out for an errand."

"No problem. Listen, they want you to come by again tomorrow."

"That's great." Caleb tries to sound enthusiastic. "I'm glad they want to see me. Is there any special reason?"

"Maybe they just like being with a younger person, and you're kind of an ambassador for the firm. I think they want to take you out to lunch. Just chat them up, okay?"

"Sure."

"Cool. I'll let you know in the morning about when to show up over there."

Golter assumes the conversation is over. But Caleb doesn't move.

"Is there something else, Caleb?"

"As you know, my mom was buried in Israel and my dad was over there for the funeral. He met an Israeli artist who apparently is doing really well. When I told him about meeting the Hobsons, he thought they might be interested in a new painting the artist wants to sell. They already own something by him. Could I tell them about the painting?"

"Sure, why not? You've seen their apartment. One thing they need is more art."

Park Avenue South and 26th Street is about thirty blocks south of the law firm, but Caleb decides to walk because the meeting isn't until seven. There's time to kill. He'll walk slowly. He could hang around the office if he wanted, where the associates will be hard at work for another three or four hours.

But he wants to get out. Maybe he'll get a slice of pizza on the way.

But what if she expects to eat? What if she wants him to buy her dinner? Lots of people in New York don't eat until after seven.

Outside the streets are jammed. It's after five o'clock. Everybody is going home from their offices. Thousands of people are wrapped up in their own little worlds.

Caleb is like them. He too is wrapped up in his own world. Does he look preoccupied? Does he look stressed? Maybe so. But if he were to tell these people about his life they would certainly understand why he's stressed. They would cheer him on.

If Orly wants to eat dinner—or even if she just wants some coffee or a glass of white wine—Caleb will of course pay the bill. He'll pay no matter what it costs. So he'd better be sure he's got enough money so his debit card doesn't bounce.

Really, he knows perfectly well that he's got enough money. But it's best to be sure. Also, if the computer system in the restaurant system crashes then his card won't work. He should take out some cash.

But here's an amazing coincidence, truly fantastic, one of the most astonishing occurrences in the history of the world.

As Caleb is about to enter a Citibank branch, he glances through the glass door and sees Orly waiting in line to use the ATM.

His heart skips a beat. He hurries off down the sidewalk.

How awkward would it have been if he'd gone into the bank and encountered Orly at a time and place where neither one of them is ready?

What would have happened? Maybe after some "what a pleasant surprise" stuff, they would have gone ahead and used the ATM. What if one of their cards was declined? Or both their cards? What then?

The possibility of following Orly after she leaves the Citibank branch—tailing her, shadowing her—never occurs to Caleb. He'll see her soon enough. She'll be at the Hotel

Giraffe. But it's only six o'clock. There's still an hour to wait. Even if he gets there fifteen minutes early, which he plans to do, there's forty-five minutes before she arrives.

He's still in shock about seeing Orly in the bank, but now he sees her in a coffee shop as he passes by the window. He's certain it's her, but he doesn't want to go back and check because he doesn't want her to see him, just as he didn't want her to see him in the bank. Also, what if she's having coffee with another man before she meets him at the Hotel Giraffe?

And then he has a moment of clarity, an absolutely lucid moment. Not long ago there had been a moment when he thought he could be going nuts, and this is another moment like that.

He walks on Third Avenue. A thousand faces fly past him. He continues walking at a slow pace. He doesn't want to start perspiring.

He takes some detours. If he passes a flower shop, he'll buy some flowers. But he doesn't pass one. He walks around in circles.

Finally, there's the Hotel Giraffe.

He's fifteen minutes early.

Good, good, good.

He enters the Hotel Giraffe. It's a small hotel, a boutique, with a lobby or reception area in which a few people are having coffee or drinks. There's leather and wood everywhere, sofas and easy chairs like an old-fashioned hotel, but there's also a trendy vibe that gives the tweedy decor an ironic it's-all-in-fun spin congruent with a hotel named the Hotel Giraffe. Whatever. And yes, this looks like a good place to talk.

He scans the lobby. Is Orly already here? If she's already

here that could be a good sign or a bad sign. But he looks around carefully and sees that she's not already here.

He takes a seat on a leather couch in a little nook with a coffee table in front of the couch and a wing-back chair beside it. She'll be able to see him when she comes in. In fact, she can't miss seeing him because the couch is in a direct line of sight from the entrance to the lobby.

The possibility that he'll get stood up never occurs to Caleb. If that thought begins to occur in his unconscious mind, some psychological mechanism prevents him from actually thinking it. His eyes are fixed on the doorway across the lobby.

Two or three times the door opens and someone enters, but not Orly. A couple walks in followed by an attractive young woman. Then the door opens again and Elijah comes in.

It's not Orly! It's Elijah!

Elijah sees Caleb. He smiles, waves, and starts quickly across the room.

He's not dressed as a street sweeper now. He's wearing a sports coat and khaki pants. He looks like a college professor.

Caleb rises and they shake hands. Then a brief hug. They sit down, Caleb on the leather couch and Elijah on the wingback chair.

"It's great to see you," Elijah says. "How have you been?"

"Pretty well. Working." Then he says, "This is a surprise."

Caleb is struggling to hide his astonishment at Elijah's shockingly unexpected appearance. But Elijah appears to believe everything's going according to plan.

A young woman appears, a server. "Can I get you anything? Would you like to see a menu?"

"Maybe I'll have tea," Elijah says. "Any kind of tea is fine."

Caleb says, "Yes, I'd like tea also."

"I'll be right back with your tea."

She turns away. Caleb thinks the server looks like Orly. Could this all be some kind of ruse?

"I've been thinking a lot about you," Elijah says. "I mean, the last time I saw you it was a little weird. You had just fainted or something. Things can get that way when you're stressed out."

"Yeah, I guess so," Caleb says.

Elijah is listening intently. Without rising, he pulls the wing-back chair closer to Caleb. "Tell me honestly, Caleb. How are you doing? What's been going on?"

"I'm getting more attention at the law firm, but I'm still not that interested in the law. I took the LSAT, and I probably bombed it. For me, the law firm is just a temporary job. I'm ready to stop at any moment. The problem is, I have to know what I want to do next, and I have to be able to explain that to my dad."

Elijah says, "Go on. Is there more?"

"There's more, but it's all connected. Both my father and my uncle are really in a hurry for me to find a wife, which means having a career to support her. They expect me to do it right away."

"Who is your uncle? I don't think you've mentioned him before."

"Uncle Maish. I give my uncle a lot of credit. He's worked all his life to make his jewelry business a big success. It's kind of ironic how he feels about me, because he never married. His business is his family."

Elijah thinks for a moment, taking this in. Then he asks, "How does all that make you feel?"

"I was kind of getting used to dealing with them. But I've changed since my mother died. It's like things are happening completely outside my control. That's how I felt about her death, and now that's how everything feels."

Caleb continues, "I don't feel like my mom abandoned me. I feel abandoned by the One Who allowed this to happen, or even caused it to happen. I feel abandoned by God."

Elijah nods. "First of all, whether you realize it or not, you're here right now because at the level of your soul you've made a decision to listen to the Divine voice. That's a big step forward. The decisions we make at every moment take us either backward or forward, and you're going forward. I'm absolutely sure of that."

This seems like a grand pronouncement to Caleb. He isn't sure how to respond. Elijah's presence is so strong that it almost overshadows Caleb's complete puzzlement over what Elijah is doing there in the first place. Why is Elijah there instead of Orly? He urgently wants to ask about this.

Before he can find the words, however, Elijah goes on: "None of this is easy, but here's a story that might help. It's not really a story. More like a metaphor. Picture a mother who sends her child out to play in the backyard. The mother stays in the kitchen, and the child can see her in the window. They smile at each other. It's all going great. But suppose the mother were to pull the window blinds shut for a minute. Now the child only sees a closed shade. It's really scary. But of course the mother never stops looking through the cracks. The mother never stops watching, loving, and caring."

For Caleb, it's amazing how much meaning Elijah brings to such a simple story. At least for a moment, Caleb feels something begin to lift inside himself. A weight that has been there since his mother's death slowly gives way to the start of comfort and hope.

And Elijah isn't done yet. "Caleb, you aren't alone. Every person that descends into this world is challenged by a struggle between body and soul, between darkness and light. We can, of course, lament the darkness, but concentrating on that is a dangerous mistake. Our true purpose is to discover and reveal the light in ourselves and in the world around us.

"We're born with the capacity to find the hidden light and to make it visible again. This is my purpose in life, Caleb. It's why I'm here in Times Square. It's your purpose too, maybe in a law firm, with whomever you meet and where you are. I want to help you see that. Our collective task is to reveal the light."

Elijah is so intense. He looks at life from such a vast perspective. This might have seemed to diminish Caleb's problems, as if they're small in comparison. But Elijah's intention is the exact opposite of that. He's saying that concepts like great or small don't exist in our spiritual mission. Everything is an opportunity—also an obligation—to reveal the light.

Elijah senses that it might be more than Caleb bargained for in this visit. With a smile, he puts his hand on Caleb's shoulder. "It's important to see the big picture first. But I'm sure you've got some specific things you need to talk about."

"Yes."

"We can talk about those things now if you want." Elijah's voice is gentle.

"I came here to meet Orly."

"Orly." He doesn't say it as a question. It's just a statement of fact. He says it again. "Orly."

"I was with her at your place in Times Square. I was with her when I passed out and you found me."

Elijah nods, "Of course, Caleb, I know Orly very well."

"You do? I was supposed to meet her but you're here instead. Do you have any idea what happened?"

Elijah pauses. Then, "Caleb, I am sending you on a mission, but it's really no different from the mission we are on when our souls enter our bodies at birth. The mission is to reveal God in yourself and in the world. It's learning that God is with you every minute of every day."

Caleb can't stand to hear any more of this. In a desperate whisper he says, "I came here to meet Orly!"

As the server returns with two cups of tea, Elijah calmly takes a pen from his pocket and begins printing some numbers on a napkin.

The server departs. Still desperate, Caleb says, "Elijah!" To his own surprise, it sounds like a demand now.

Elijah passes the napkin to Caleb. He says, "You're going to Israel. I think I told you that was going to happen. You're going to Safed."

"That's where my mother is buried."

"Many sages are also there, Caleb. When you're in Safed, call the number on the napkin. You'll meet the Reb."

"The Reb?"

"The author of *The Secret of the Light*."

Without further explanation, Elijah stands up. "It's great to see you, Caleb. Good luck. Shalom."

Caleb stands also. "You're leaving? What about Orly?"

"I believe she's getting married to an Israeli artist."

"What!"

Elijah says, "This is for you."

He takes an envelope from inside his jacket and hands it to Caleb, then turns quickly and walks back toward the door.

Of course, Caleb immediately tears open the envelope. There's only a brief note printed on a small piece of lined paper. It's not even folded:

> *You'll see me again when you really want me.*
> *When you really need me you'll find me or*
> *else I'll find you!*

Caleb visits P.L. Tuck and Company, the jewelry store founded by Maish's father fifty years ago. Maish had started working at the store when he was in grade school. It's the one place in the world where he seems to feel at home. He spends as much time as he can at the business and sometimes even sleeps on a folding cot in a corner of his office.

As he greets Caleb in his office, Maish says, "Caleb, what happened? Orly was looking for you."

Caleb cannot believe what he is hearing.

"I did not see her. In fact, my friend Elijah showed up instead and he told me that Ory is getting married!"

"Caleb, wait a minute. Who are you talking about? Orly told me she was there. "

Maish pauses and ponders. "Caleb, what does the Orly that you had in mind look like?"

Caleb cannot get her out of his mind. "She has green eyes, fair skin, and dark hair."

"Aha!" Maish exhales. "You were looking for the wrong one! The Orly I set you up with has blonde hair and blue eyes."

Caleb catches his breath.

"Uncle Maish, I cannot believe it! I met a woman. . . ." Caleb realizes his uncle would not understand and pauses mid-sentence. The worst thing about his meeting was learning from Elijah that his Orly was getting married and it was not worth explaining everything.

"Caleb, it happens," Maish comforts Caleb. "Shake it off. There is something I do want to speak to you about. Can you focus?"

"Yes," Caleb mournfully responds.

"Great. I know Sam wants you to be a lawyer, but I'd love to teach you the jewelry business. You can't be all things to all people is the first thing you need to know. That's why my niche is the military and the police. Firemen too. Those people love to be catered to because most of the time they don't get the respect they deserve."

He goes on, "Have I ever told you how this business actually works? Have I ever really explained it to you? Let's talk about mail order. First I run a big ad in an Army or Navy magazine. Here's the offer: they can send away for an engagement ring with a price of five hundred dollars. But then it says, 'If you're in the active duty military, you only pay three hundred dollars.' And then there's another little thing that says, 'If you send the coupon in before Thanksgiving, it only costs you two hundred dollars.' I run that ad maybe six weeks before Thanksgiving, like in the October issue of the magazine."

Caleb has heard this many times before. But he says, "That's great, Uncle Maish. Really smart."

"Of course, the ring they get only costs me fifty dollars at the most, so if I sell it for two hundred that's what we call a double keystone markup. It's the wholesale price times four. All by mail order. Of course, the way we sell engagement rings in person is completely different."

Maish could go on like this for a very long time. There are moments when he seems to be winding down, but then he gets his second wind. His jewelry business is the love of his life.

"I'll tell you something else. You've probably already heard this but bear with me. For some reason, and after thousands of people have passed through these doors, not one of them has ever come out and asked me, 'Who is P.L. Tuck?' Nobody has ever asked that. It's a good thing too, because there is no P.L. Tuck! There never was and there never will be, and how my father came up with the name P.L. Tuck is a story in itself."

Suddenly, as if stung by a bee, he glances at his watch. "Hey, you caught me at a funny time. I'm expecting an important call from Italy. This will be one of the most important calls I've ever gotten. You see, there are two types of jewelry that my clientele wants. They always have and they always will. They want engagement rings, and they want gold chains to hang around their necks. For the general population gold chains are kind of a fad that comes and goes. But for policemen, firemen, soldiers, sailors, they consistently want gold chains."

He looks at Caleb expectantly. Caleb nods. "I understand."

"The call I'm waiting for is from a guy at one of the largest gold chain manufacturers in Italy. He's going to sell me gold chains straight from the factory. Fourteen carats, no gold-plated *dreck*. No middleman. He's doing this at great risk to himself. It's off the books. If he gets caught it's curtains. I have to pay cash. I have to buy in volume. But there's no middleman marking up the goods, because that's what kills you."

"Right."

Now a discreet but insistent chime arises from the phone on Maish's desk. He reaches for it but then quickly glances at Caleb. "Could you wait outside for a bit, Caleb? This is the big call. It just makes me nervous if there's somebody here."

"Sure, Maish. I'll be outside."

"Thanks, buddy."

The door closes behind Caleb. Maish answers the phone.

In the waiting room outside Maish's office, there's a desk for a secretary. But as he sits in a chair against the wall, Caleb realizes that Maish has never had a secretary. In fact, in the roughly half-dozen times Caleb has been to Maish's store over the years, the secretary's desk has never changed in the slightest detail. The chair behind the desk has always been positioned in exactly the same angle. It has never moved an inch.

This is typical of Maish, and so much the opposite of Sam. Caleb's father is cautious and deliberate, always trying to minimize risk, carefully considering every detail. Maish is flamboyant and impatient, a hustler in every sense of the word. They both mean well, but by different paths they still end up with their fair share of anxiety, or even misery. If a certain level of misery is an inevitable fact of human life, there's a greater need for rabbis and Torah scholars than lawyers or jewelers in Caleb's opinion. He's certain of that, but what his role should be is still unclear.

In a shorter time than Caleb expects, Maish comes out of his office. There's a look of fulfillment and generosity in his eyes. His business deal has become a life-changing experience.

He says, "The deal is going through!"

Suddenly Maish grins at Caleb as if noticing him for the first time. "Hey, it's great to see you, kid! Let me show you around the store. Of course, nothing much has changed since the last time you were here, whenever that was. I can't even remember. The physical plant is irrelevant anyway. Except for the engagement rings, I could close the store tomorrow and still do a big business just with mail order. I'm probably the only one in the industry who can say that. But let's take a walk around. Why not?"

"The gold chain deal is a game changer. Do you know how much I stand to make on this?"

"I don't know."

"Take a wild guess."

"A million dollars."

"Yes! A million dollars!" Maish laughs again. "I'm going to make a million dollars with gold chains straight from the manufacturer in Italy! Good luck with your women!"

Caleb has not seen Marvin for a while, so he's glad to see him again in their office the morning after his enigmatic meeting with Elijah and his unsatisfying conversation with Maish.

"Hey, long time no see," Marvin says with a grin. "I've missed you. What's been going on?"

"Well, I'm learning a lot," Caleb says.

"Great. I'm learning a lot from Butenhamer too,"

Marvin says. "It's like I'm a lawyer already. In the old days all anybody had to do was take the bar exam and pass it. You could just walk in off the street, take the exam, and be a lawyer. I don't know if law schools even existed. Abe Lincoln never went to law school. But you've been working with Golter, right? What's that like?"

"Well, Golter's got me hanging out with an elderly couple who bring the firm a lot of billable work. All I have to do is deliver papers for them to sign and admire their art collection. I don't think they really care about legal stuff. Their whole life is art collecting."

"What kind of art?"

"Everything you could possibly imagine. They've got a huge apartment and it's basically an art gallery. Every room has a different style or theme."

Then he says, "Marvin, my dad wants me to tell them about an artist he met in Israel. The artist wants to sell a painting. I doubt they'll be interested, but Golter said I should tell them."

"Tell them then. They definitely won't be interested if they don't know about it."

Caleb is at the Hobson's apartment.

Looking at a Picasso pencil drawing, Danvers says, "You can recognize a good artist, let alone a great artist, by a confident line. See how this single line goes from her eyebrow all the way down to her knee? It's done exactly right, and you can bet he did it on the first try. Picasso was a guy who didn't need erasers on his pencils."

"His father was an artist too," Mouse says. "But when his father saw how talented little Pablo was, he gave up painting. Or so the story goes."

They've been on a tour of the apartment for nearly an hour and the tour is nowhere near finished. This has been much more detailed than Caleb's first tour, with sharper attention to specific works.

Caleb remarks, "You also collect new artists, right? Contemporary artists?"

"Of course, if something catches our eye," Mouse replies. She looks at Caleb with new interest. "Are you an artist, by the way?"

"No, definitely not. But the other day you mentioned Yehoshua Gips."

"Of course, the wonderful Israeli artist. We have one of his Hebrew letters. Are you familiar with his work?"

"Well, just a little."

"He's becoming well-known," Danvers says. "He could probably become even better known if he made more of an effort. But being under the radar is part of his appeal. People like to feel that they're discovering somebody."

Caleb says, "My father met him in Israel. He's doing something on the letter *aleph*."

"The letter *aleph*?" Mouse asks. She's immediately fascinated. "Is it a painting?"

Caleb tries to remember what Sam told him about Gips' project. "I think it's a painting. A big one."

Danvers and Mouse are waiting for Caleb to say more.

"He wants to do a private sale, not through a gallery. He wants to find someone who really connects with the letter aleph. That's what my father told me."

Danvers is skeptical. "How do you connect with the letter *aleph*?"

"The *aleph* is definitely an interesting letter," Caleb says. He feels more confident speaking about the Hebrew alphabet than about art or artists. "Sometimes it's a silent letter and sometimes it's not."

He adds, "So maybe the *aleph* is sort of like God. He's been silent for a while, but He wasn't always silent and maybe He won't be silent forever."

"Maybe we'll still be here when He finally breaks His silence," Mouse teases. "Successful artists do try to avoid selling through a gallery so they don't have to pay the commission. It's really simple for everybody."

Danvers says, "If you have a contact with him, maybe you can mention that you know a collector who's interested in his work. Don't say anything about money," he adds, with a wink.

Caleb calls Sam that night. "Hi Dad," he says, "you know the art collectors I'm working with? I told them about the artist."

"Yehoshua Gips," Sam says. "Were they interested?"

"They were."

Sam is excited. "What did I tell you! I had a hunch. What do they want to do?"

"They want me to contact him and say that I know someone who might be interested."

"Did they say you should contact him or that I should contact him?"

"Maybe you should do it."

"You told them about me, right?"

"I told them how you met Yehoshua Gips in Israel."

"Okay, I'll call him. Goodbye."

Sam sets his alarm to wake up at 5:00 a.m. so he can call Yehoshua around lunch time in Israel. He hesitates and resets his alarm for 7:00 a.m. as calling that early would seem too anxious.

The next morning, he dials Yehoshua. Yehoshua answers with a few words in Hebrew. Sam says, "Hi, it's Sam."

"Good morning, Sam! How are you doing?"

"I'm fine, everything's good. Listen, the reason I'm calling is because there are some people in New York, art collectors, husband and wife . . ."

He stops. He should have thought this through more carefully before he called. Why was he in such a hurry to call? What got into him? But it's too late now. He has to go on.

"Anyway, my son works at a law firm, and he met these big art collectors. Their whole apartment is full of art. They were talking about art with my son, and he happened to mention that his father met Yehoshua Gips in Israel. They were very impressed because they know about you already. They're very interested."

After a pause Yehoshua Gips says, "When you say they're interested, you mean they want to buy?"

"I think so. Yes."

There's a longer pause. Sam is really worried. He may have crossed some invisible line by trying to talk about buying and selling art with Yehoshua Gips. What if Yehoshua Gips asks for the names of the big art collectors? Sam doesn't even know their names. But he has no choice. He had to strike while the iron was hot.

Now, however, there's the sound of Yehoshua Gips laughing. He's joyfully laughing on the telephone. He laughs for at least ten seconds and then says, "Sam, I'm so happy you called! Everything is wonderful and I'm very excited about the big art collectors. But first I have to give you some great news. I'm getting married!"

"Oh, that really is wonderful, Yehoshua. I'm so happy for you. Mazel tov, mazel tov!"

"Yes, mazel tov indeed. I feel very blessed. She's a wonderful young woman."

Sam tries to think of what to say next. The main thing is, he's got to seem enthusiastic, and eventually the conversation might get back to the big art collectors."

Sam says, "When?"

"When? You mean when am I getting married?"

"Yes."

"Soon, soon. I wish it could be today. But very soon. In two weeks."

"Well, mazel tov. Will it be a big wedding?"

"I hope so! Will you come?"

A bit uneasily, Sam laughs. "Of course I'll come. Thank you for the invitation."

"I'm serious. Just jump on a plane. Bring your son. Bring your little daughter. You told me you have a little daughter."

"Sure."

Yehoshua Gips is obviously in a very expansive mood. Getting him back onto the topic of art might be impossible now. Also, the whole business of bringing Caleb and Nora to Israel has come out of nowhere.

Somehow Yehoshua Gips senses hesitation on Sam's part. He says, "Listen, Sam, if the cost of tickets and stuff is a concern, I'll be happy to reimburse you. I just really want you to come."

"No, no, no, the tickets are no problem," Sam says

emphatically.

Yehoshua Gips adds, "Also, I know it's very soon after your wife's passing. Is it too soon for you to attend a joyous celebration? I just really want you to be there on this special occasion. "

"I'll come and Caleb and Nora will come too, as you mentioned. Definitely. They can be present for the ceremony but will have to refrain from celebrating at the festive meal since they are still in mourning."

"I understand, of course. Here's another idea. We can kill two birds with one stone. Let's get the big art collectors to come, too."

"Sure, why not?"

"They can see the painting. We'll find time a few days before the wedding for talking business. Can you take care of that?"

"Sure."

"Wonderful. I've got to run. Keep in touch. Let me know the plan. Get everybody over here in the next ten days. Send me the bill. It's going to be great."

"Absolutely, and mazel tov again."

PART THREE

The flight from JFK to Ben Gurion airport will take twelve hours.

The brief security interview in the ticket line at JFK goes quickly and smoothly. There's a podium where an attendant asks a few security questions of every passenger.

It seems routine to Caleb. He's been to Israel before. Also, everything makes sense to him now. There are still a few loose ends, but basically it makes sense. And he has a plan.

Nora is also quite calm, at least outwardly. But Danvers seems offended when he returns to the ticket line.

"The guy asked me if I had any family in Israel. I told him that I certainly do have family. The whole human race is my family!"

As they relax in the waiting area, Danvers offers some advice. "When we flew to Australia we sat next to a gentleman who showed us how to prevent jet lag. It works like a charm. Do you want to know what it is?"

Caleb says, "I certainly do."

"As soon as you get on the plane you close your eyes, and you don't open your eyes again until you get to the destination." Danvers closes his eyes. "If you fall asleep, that's even better."

Danvers adds, "The only time I'll open my eyes is if I have to use the bathroom."

"Maybe I'll give it a try," Caleb says.

Mouse adds, "I sleep like a log."

Nora, who is sitting next to Mouse in the waiting area, turns to her and asks, "Sleep like a log. That's just an expression, right?"

"Yes."

"Can I ask you one question?"

"Of course you can?"

"How do you get your money?"

Mouse looks down at Nora. Mouse is touched by the look of frank and honest inquiry on Nora's face. It's actually the same look that Mouse gets on her own face when she asks Caleb questions about Judaism.

She smiles at Nora and says, "Whenever a dairy farm uses our invention, we get money."

About an hour later, the plane is backing up from the gate. Although he's managed to conceal it so far, Caleb is a nervous wreck. Nervous wreck is a phrase his mom would use sometimes, like if the stove wouldn't work or something. Now Caleb is a nervous wreck.

He murmurs the Twenty-Third Psalm, the prayer for all occasions. As always, it calms him. He's read and recited it many times in his life, but he's never really thought closely about the words. The words used to just flow by themselves.

"One other thing," Danvers says, with his eyes still closed. "I may snore. I apologize if that happens. Do you have earplugs?"

"No, I don't. Maybe I should have thought of that."

"It's one thing we've learned in our travels. Don't leave home without them."

But the possibility of sleeping, the whole idea of sleeping, is the farthest thing from Caleb's mind.

Caleb gets his carry-on bag from under the seat and removes his black notebook. He opens a page that he had written a few days after his mom passed while sitting *shiva*.

When we all sat around the table on Friday night to recite the blessings over the wine . . . you were not there. We could not help but cry as we looked at the empty seat at the table. As we sang the Ode to the Woman of Valor, Dad shared how lucky he was to have a wife like you, it was a taste of Heaven on earth.

I could have been a better son. I helped you on the first Friday night upon returning from studying in Israel. Why didn't I help again? We always take people for granted until we do not have them.

The world is cold, and your warmth is not here.

It is so important for me to remember to be the person you wanted me to be.

I wish sometimes all the people around the house would disappear and only you would be back. Simply to be near you, to tell you I love you and give you a big hug and talk to you and never take anything for granted.

My heart is aching. I will miss you always and will always love you. I feel so lucky for the time I had with you. You always reminded me to be sensitive to others, to walk people to the door. You became very upset if I neglected to do a kind deed. Clearing the table should never have been a burden. You always told me that it was a blessing.

You did not ask me to do things for you but to educate me. I do not understand why God took you away. Why? I cannot believe it is real.

Since you're gone, my world has turned upside down forever. I can't accept that people are going on with their lives as if nothing happened. That makes me very angry.

Yes, it makes Caleb angry that people are just going on with their lives. But something else also makes him angry, and he'd better admit it to himself. His obsession with Orly also makes him angry now. But there's no escape from that, at least not for more than a few minutes.

Writing to his mom is an escape. He turns to another page in his notebook. It's the page where he lists his sightings of Orly since the first time they met in Times Square. The list is a page of small writing in the notebook but it's actually incomplete. He feels like there were more sightings.

To get his mind off Orly he wants to write another letter to Elyse in the notebook. But he writes a letter to Orly instead.

Dear Orly,
Whenever I think of you now, I automatically think of Yehoshua Gips also. I've never met Yehoshua Gips and I don't really know that much about him, but I imagine that since you are going to marry him he must be a remarkable man. I do know that he likely

*will be rich, because if he sells his artwork to people
like Danvers and Mouse then he's got a lot of money.*
    *Is that what attracts you to him, at least in
part?*
    *I don't see Yehoshua Gips as a bad person just
as I don't see you as bad for being attracted to him.*

The plane lands. Everyone is tired, although everyone
except Caleb has slept. Standing around waiting for the
suitcases to appear in the baggage claim area, there's not
much conversation. Finally the suitcases appear. Caleb finds
a cart for the suitcases. Then the journey begins to the exit
where a shuttle will take them to the hotel.

"How long will the drive be tomorrow?" Mouse asks.
Her voice is less cheerful than usual.

Danvers says, "It shouldn't take long at all. A couple of
hours."

"A couple of hours!" Mouse is incredulous.

Danvers wonders how he has become the travel agent
and social director on this trip. Usually when he and Mouse
travel they work together like a well-oiled machine. Usually
Danvers makes the plane reservations while Mouse arranges
for hotels, unless they are staying with friends or relatives.
They had once gone on a cruise around the Caribbean, which
had been disappointing. There was nothing to do except eat.
They had laughed about it and had continued eating.

Eventually the shuttle arrives.

In the hotel lobby, everyone agrees it's time for a nap even if
it's morning in Israel.

"We'll meet here tomorrow morning," Sam says. He

starts fussing with a problem on his suitcase in order to avoid getting in the elevator with Danvers and Mouse. Caleb half-expects to see Orly among the travelers in the lobby, but she's not there. Or maybe he just doesn't see her.

Sam has made sure the drive to Safed is as comfortable as possible. In America the transporting vehicle would be called a party bus, but Sam just calls it a car. It comes with a driver who speaks almost no English.

With the car on the road, Mouse is rested and back to her old self. She says, "Well, this is very exciting, and I can't wait to see the piece. And of course, it will be an honor to meet Yehoshua Gips. You're a friend of his, isn't that right?" she says to Sam.

"I don't really know him that well. We met by accident when I was in Israel after my wife passed away."

Danvers says, "He seems to have done extremely well for himself. His work sells for a lot of money. Of course, what's a lot of money to some people is not a lot of money to other people."

Yehoshua Gips's gallery, his studio, and his living space are all in one building. Upon the arrival of his guests, Yehoshua Gips provides a light lunch in a dining room hung with framed pictures of some of his drawings and etchings.

He says, "When I lived in London I used to visit the National Gallery in Trafalgar Square, and my favorite pictures were the Rembrandts. When I first saw Rembrandt's works, they reminded me of a legend about the creation of light. When God first created an overwhelmingly powerful light, it was so strong that people could see from one end of the universe to the other, and even from the present moment to the end of time. God was afraid that the wicked might abuse that powerful light, so He hid it away until the Messiah comes. But now and then there are great souls who are blessed to access that light, and I think Rembrandt was one of them. The light in his pictures is the light that was first created by God."

"What role does light play in your pictures?" Mouse asks, reverently.

Yehoshua Gips laughs. "It might seem that light plays very little role in my work, since my paintings are just black letters on a white background. But Light is really the fundamental energy in all my work—spiritual light, that is. That's how I feel about Orly, too. She really is the Light of my life in the sense that she literally makes my life possible, just as the black letters of the Torah are only possible because of the white foundation that they rest upon."

Yehoshua Gips hesitates. He glances around the table. Has he said the wrong thing? Has he gone too far? But Danvers, Mouse, and even Sam seem to understand and appreciate this conversation with a real artist. Danvers and Mouse have of course spoken with artists before, but never with an intensely Jewish one living in Israel.

Listening to this, however, it would be impossible for Caleb to find words that express his pain and complete dismay. What on earth could Caleb have done to deserve what he's hearing? Has he sinned greatly?

And he's trapped. They're seated around a table in a back room of the artist's studio, with Caleb furthest from the door. A light lunch has been served by one of the artist's several apprentices. A dozen paintings, some finished and others still in progress, are leaning against the walls. Classical music plays softly on a radio.

"I can hardly believe all the blessings I've experienced in my life," says Yehoshua Gips. "I grew up in an observant home in Northbrook, a mostly Jewish suburb of Chicago. I went through the motions of Jewish life: Friday night meals for the Sabbath, the holidays, a bar mitzvah. I was also used to the trappings of an upper middle class suburban existence. But somehow, thank God, I sensed there was more. There was an inner yearning that ignited my personal journey."

"You've used the word *ignited*," says Danvers. "It's a word that suggests something specific happening at a certain point in time. Was there a moment when you felt that ignition taking place?"

Yehoshua Gips thinks for a moment. "I had been a student in psychology at Ohio State University, and then attended the School of the Art Institute in Chicago. I had never been interested in meditation, which I'd always thought of as an Eastern spiritual practice. Then one day I picked up a book by Rabbi Aryeh Kaplan that introduced me to the whole tradition of Jewish meditation. I started to think about painting as a form of visual meditation, a mental discipline for connecting with the viewers of a painting, and even connecting with God."

What an eloquent statement this is. There needs to be some acknowledgement of it, some expression of respect. But no one has any idea what to say. There's a sense of inadequacy in the presence of this artist who, although he's still a young man, seems to have it all. He's intelligent, creative, wealthy, and authentically spiritual.

He's also sensitive to the feelings of others, and he's aware that Caleb is not quite on the same frequency as the rest of the people at the table.

Yehoshua Gips looks toward Caleb with a gently inquisitive expression. "Caleb, what about you?" he says. "Has there ever been a moment when you started to see things in a different way? When you felt like the world had changed, and you had changed with it?"

Much to his own surprise, Caleb hears himself reply without the slightest hesitation.

"Yes, I have moments like that. But it wasn't just a moment. I feel like it's still going on."

"Really? Wow. Do you think you could tell us about that?"

"He's going to talk about his bar mitzvah," Sam jokes, but Caleb has already begun to speak.

"I met someone who got me to question things that I had just accepted without really understanding them. It happened quite recently, just after my mother died. I was feeling pretty weak and vulnerable, but I realized that I'm actually different than I thought I was. Stronger and more determined."

"Determined?" asks Yehoshua Gips. "Determined to accomplish something?"

"Determined to reveal the light."

Yehoshua Gips smiles. "That's beautiful. Just beautiful." He looks toward Sam. "You must be very proud of your son."

Sam takes a deep breath and nods. "I am proud. But . . ."

"Yes, I'm determined to reveal the light, and there's something else too," Caleb interjects. "I have to be together with my soulmate, no matter what it takes."

Once more, Yahoshua Gips says, "Wow." Then he says it again. "Wow. I know exactly how you feel, and I feel the same way. But as you may know, finding and uniting with your soulmate is as great a miracle as the parting of the Red Sea. That's why I feel so blessed. Not being able to see my bride for seven days before the wedding is extremely difficult. But I have to obey the teachings, because the miraculous teachings are what brought us together."

Danvers pipes up. "Mouse and I recently celebrated our fiftieth anniversary, so we certainly understand the beautiful feelings you've expressed, and we wish you all the happiness in the world."

"Yes, yes," Mouse chips in.

"Meanwhile, we would love to see your work. Could we step into the gallery?"

"Of course!" says Yehoshua Gips, getting quickly to his feet. "Let's have a look . . ."

Yehoshua Gips's gallery is a large room whose walls are hung with paintings, etchings, and pencil or charcoal drawings. All of them depict Hebrew letters, sometimes an individual letter, or the same letter repeated from different angles and in different sizes, or sometimes groups of three letters. But there are no colors. Black and white is Yehoshua Gips' signature palette.

Gesturing toward the walls, Yehoshua Gips says, "Each of my works is a map of a spiritual landscape. Each one is a visual representation of an invisible reality. One is about love. Another is about the presence of God everywhere in our lives. They're all narratives to explain a deeper meaning."

While Danvers and Mouse listen attentively, Sam is only halfway paying attention. What in the world had Caleb meant with that soulmate business? Had he met a woman? Maybe it was a woman at the law firm. Not a secretary, but a lawyer in her own right. If she's a lawyer in her own right, she will be making enough money so that Caleb can study Torah if that's what he really wants to do. Let him get it out of his system. Then, eventually, he will go to law school after all. Through it all, they'll have a nanny to take care of the children.

Yehoshua Gips continues, "Our ultimate goal in this lifetime is to strengthen our relationships with our fellow human beings, as well as our connection with God. Obviously those forms of connection are different to some extent, but they both come into being by doing everything we can to bring goodness into the world. Life brings us all kinds of experiences, both positive and negative. Our task is to find the blessing in every situation. Sometimes the blessings are clearly revealed, sometimes they're hidden from view. But every experience is an opportunity for the soul to come to a place that will find infinite goodness."

Like Sam, Caleb's thoughts are elsewhere as Yehoshua Gips is speaking. A plan has taken shape in Caleb's mind. The plan is rather vague at first, but soon it starts to gain sharper focus. At first it is an idea, a concept. Then it becomes a series of images in full detail, like scenes in a film.

Caleb has only attended a few weddings in his life, and none recently, but he seems to remember a moment in which the groom places the veil over the bride's face right before the procession. This is the moment in which Caleb will step forward and disclose the ordained connection, the soulmate relationship, that exists between himself and Orly. Caleb realizes he does not know for sure that Yehoshua is marrying Orly but what other artist could it be. Elijah did tell him that Orly is marrying an artist in Israel.

Caleb knows he'll need to think a lot more about this plan between now and the wedding. He'll flesh it out. He'll connect the dots. But the basic idea is there.

Danvers and Mouse are eager to see the *aleph* painting right away. That's why they've made the long trip to Israel and so far they're glad they've made the trip. Yehoshua Gips and the examples of his work they've seen so far are everything they could have wanted. They're ready for the main course, which is the *aleph* painting. They feel drawn toward it.

Yehoshua Gips also feels a surge of energy. He says, "Something strange and inspirational is taking place now. I know you'd like to see the *aleph* painting as soon as possible. But here's the thing. Maybe it's because I've been talking about ideas that are so important to me, but I feel a need to do a bit more work on the painting. When I have a feeling like that—and I wish it happened more often—it's important for me to act on it right away. I can certainly show you the painting, and maybe you'd even enjoy watching me put some finishing touches on it. Does that appeal to you?"

Danvers glances at the others, then enthusiastically nods. "We would feel honored to see a true artist at work. We'll even sign a non-disclosure agreement if you wish."

"Oh, that won't be necessary, you can disclose whatever you want," Yehoshua Gips laughs as he leads the way through a side door in the gallery beyond which another world lies.

It's the birthing room of art in all its grand messiness and squalor. The white-walled gallery has a rather severe vibration, like a scientific laboratory in which finished paintings are displayed in a climate-controlled environment. But here in the back room cans of paint are piled up against the walls along with dozens of bottles of paint thinner and who knows what else. Huge splashes of dried paint cover the linoleum floor, which could be called a work of art by itself if it could somehow be framed. But everything in the room, which is quite large, is subordinate to a gigantic beige-colored canvas adorned with a single Hebrew letter, an *aleph*. In the background there are blurry depictions of other vaguely defined forms.

As he's done hundreds of times, Yehoshua Gips switches on a paint-splashed DVD player that's on the floor in one corner of the room. The DVD player, he explains, is essential to his work. It starts blasting a mysterious Sephardic vocal performance.

"In order to work I need this DVD player," Yehoshua Gips explains. He lowers the volume. "The music and the art co-exist in a symbiotic relationship."

Danvers and Mouse are in awe of what they're witnessing. Caleb feels nauseated. Sam is mystified, as if he's landed on Mars. But Yehoshua Gips is absolutely at home here. He's mixing paint on a messy palette with the same reflex motion that he used to turn on the DVD player.

"The *aleph*, the *aleph*," Yehoshua Gips intones, standing before the enormous painting like a matador in front of a bull. The paintbrush is his sword.

Still smiling, and with his eyes still on the painting, Yehoshua Gips addresses Danvers. "Danvers, disintermediation is a concept that's become important to me. It means doing away with the middleman. When I started out, getting a gallery to represent me was a dream come true. But now a gallery is an albatross around my neck."

He adds some more paint to the *aleph*. "The gallery takes half, and for what?"

"It's the same way with an auction," Danvers agrees. "Christie's takes their cut and it comes out of my pocket."

"That's why I want to do a sale outside the gallery system," Yehoshua Gips says. "I'm going to do a series of large *aleph* paintings in different color schemes. It'll be like the paintings that Rothko did at the end of his life, the ones that are in Houston. This is the first one, so obviously it will be the most valuable. Those Rothko paintings were funded by the de Menil family. Do you see what I'm getting at, Danvers?" he asks.

"Well, I can do five hundred thousand for this one."

"I was thinking two million."

"Oh, all right." Danver agrees without little hesitation.

"Great. Thank you, Danvers."

Yehoshua Gips turns away from the painting. He looks at Mouse. "We're starting a partnership, a relationship. I'm going to do a suite of these paintings and I'll even dedicate them to you, just like Picasso named the Vollard suite for his art dealer. But unlike the Vollard suite, there will only be one set of the *aleph* paintings. As the number of paintings grows, the value of the whole set will grow exponentially. It will be the Rothko paintings and the de Menil family. I'll be Rothko, and you'll be de Menil."

Danvers and Mouse return to their hotel. Yehoshua Gips's wedding is tomorrow, so they'll just have a room service dinner tonight and get some rest. Sam and Caleb are going to leave too, but Yehoshua Gips asks them to stay for a cup of tea.

"Would you like a cup of tea?" he asks Nora.

"Yes, of course I would."

The tea arrives and everyone mumbles blessings.

Yehoshua Gips says, "I want to apologize for how you heard me speaking just now."

Sam says, "There's nothing to be sorry about. This is how you make your living. Business is business."

"Sure. But I know how it looks when the guy offers half a million dollars for a painting and I say I want two million and incredibly enough he goes for it. But he can afford it, and I know he can afford it. Those people are big collectors. Their story is well-known. They don't have to hustle. Somebody hustled for them a long time ago. Now they get money every time a dairy farm licenses their patent. I'm not at that point. I still have to hustle. What about you?"

"Well, I'm an attorney," Sam says rather sheepishly.

Caleb says, "Maish is a hustler."

"Who's Maish?"

"That's my brother-in-law. He's in the jewelry business. Yes, he is a hustler."

Yehoshua Gips rises from the table. "Excuse me for just a second. There's something I need to take care of before I forget about it."

Sam takes advantage of this moment alone with Caleb. "This is what I've been telling you. He's an artist and a businessman at the same time."

"Right," Caleb answers. "His head is in the clouds but his feet are on the ground."

He's trying to humor Sam, but Sam misses the irony. "That's exactly correct."

In a moment Yehoshua Gips returns with something in his hand. It looks like a check. He sits down, keeping the check in his hand.

"When I talk to people about money, I think about how

I'm going to spend the money, that's for sure. That's the only way I can bring myself to have those conversations. This one was a good one because I won't be giving half the money to a gallery. That was a motivator, and it was also the biggest sale I've ever made. Did you see how he just wrote a check right on the spot?"

"Is that the check?" Sam inquires.

Yehoshua Gips laughs. "No, I didn't bring Danvers's check out here to show it to you. This is a different check."

He hands the check to Nora, who seems frightened by it. Nora slides it across the table between Caleb and Sam. Their eyes widened. It's a check for a million dollars. The "payable to" line is blank.

"When I think about what I can do with the money during a negotiation, what I'm really thinking about is how I can give it away. I don't really need money. There aren't a lot of expenses involved in making art. Brushes, paint, canvas, paper, that's about it. It's kind of magical. I do a painting, which I would do anyway, and I get money for it. The best part is giving it away, like I'm doing right now with you. Except this isn't really giving it away. It's a fifty percent commission for bringing me the buyer. That's what the gallery would get. Fair is fair."

At the hotel that night Sam sleeps with the check beside his pillow. The night table isn't close enough. Lying awake on the room's other bed, Caleb listens to his father's peaceful snoring. Perhaps he's dreaming about the check.

Sam believes this money will change his life. Those are his last words before he falls asleep. In the dark room he says, "This is going to change my life." Then the snoring begins.

A terrible thought occurs to Caleb. What if Sam dies

in his sleep? As Elyse had died suddenly, Sam could also die suddenly. His last words would be, "This money is going to change my life." Would God allow that to happen? Caleb manages not to follow that thought any farther.

The night passes slowly. Or does it pass quickly? Caleb doesn't really know. He disciplines himself to avoid looking at the digital clock on the night table but finally he can't resist. It's a few minutes past four-thirty in the morning.

When the lights were first turned off the room had been completely dark. But now in the window he can already see a faint glow of morning.

Quietly—quiet as a mouse, as Elyse used to say—Caleb rises from the bed and gets dressed. He's alert to the slightest variation in Sam's snoring. He brushes his teeth, splashes some water on his face, and heads out of the room. The wedding isn't until mid-afternoon. No need for hurrying back to the hotel.

When Sam wakes after a good night's sleep, his first thought is for the check. Where is the check, and does the check actually exist? It could all be a dream, because he's had many such dreams over the years. Dreams of an armored car's door breaking open and hundred-dollar bills flying out. Dreams of finding a duffel bag full of money that criminals have hidden. Dreams of winning the lottery.

This isn't a dream. The check is right where he had left it before going to sleep. He picks it up. He looks at the front and back of the check. He turns the check upside down. He studies the signature of Yehoshua Gips.

Caleb's bed is empty. If he's not in the other room he must have gone for a walk.

And he's not in the other room.

In a magnanimous mood, Sam decides to make the check payable to Caleb. They will share the money of course —how much will go to taxes?—but he will invite Caleb to write his name on the check. It will be a moment to remember. There will also be some money for Nora.

Sam should eat something but he's not hungry. He can't eat now. There will be food at the wedding. The whole idea of eating seems irrelevant. Possibly he'll never eat again. Why should he eat? But he would like a cup of coffee.

It's almost eight o'clock. There's a coffee shop in the hotel but those places are never any good. He'll find a little cafe where he can get coffee and a roll.

Now the telephone makes a noise. Not a ring, not a beep, sort of a squirrel-like squeak. This must be how telephones ring in Israeli hotels. It wakes Nora. Peeved, she rolls over on her side.

Who could be calling? Caleb? Nora? Maish? Yehoshua Gips?

He picks up the phone. It's Maish. Sam had provided Maish with contact information in Israel but it's the middle of the night in New York. This is not good.

In all their lives Sam has never heard Maish sound so upset. He's sobbing, then he's growling like a cornered animal. He's blaming himself for the pain he's in, he's blaming others. Sam holds the phone up in the air. He can't stand having it close to his ear. Nora wakes again.

Maish screams, "They sent me *dreck*! Oh my God, Sam! They sent me garbage!"

Then in a whisper he adds, "They sent me gold-plated chains. Garbage. Gold-plated chains."

"I have no idea what you're talking about," Sam says.

"I'm a fool. An idiot."

"Tell me what happened. That's the only way I can help you."

Sam is being the voice of reason. That's always been his role with Maish. He patiently listens to Maish's weeping. Eventually Maish explains how he sent $200,000 to Italy for fourteen and eighteen carat gold chains, and they sent him garbage.

"But that's not the worst part, Sam."

"What's the worst part?"

"Remember Doctor Lander?"

"Doctor Lander?"

"The woman doctor at the hospital."

"What about her?"

"Sam, from the first moment I saw her I was attracted to her. I didn't tell you. I told no one. It was strange, because we were there saying goodbye to Elyse. But it was like getting struck by lightning. It was like an earthquake."

"Oh God, Maish."

"I wanted to get her attention."

He's crying again but he manages to go on. "I was going to make a million dollars on the gold chains. Huge markup because no middleman."

"Mazel tov," Sam says with great irony.

"I tracked her down. Carla is her first name. Carla Lander. I was concerned that she might be married but it turns out she's a widow."

"Mazel tov again."

"I tracked her down and I pledged a million dollars to the hospital."

"What! A million dollars!"

"Sam, how can you not understand this? I wanted to not only get her attention but also give one million dollars to the hospital in memory of Elyse. I wanted nothing for myself. I was going to make a million dollars on the chains and give away one million dollars.

"I wanted to impress her. And it did. I could sense her tone of voice when we met for coffee, and I told her I was going to give a million dollars to the hospital. She put me in touch with their philanthropy guy. I put it in writing."

Maish cries out, "What am I supposed to do now? Tell them I can't afford it?"

Sam hangs up on him. Nora says, "You woke me up."

In the early morning, the narrow cobblestoned streets of Safed are at their most beautiful. Tourist shops in the area of the hotel aren't open yet, and Caleb quickly makes his way to the older area of this ancient town. It's so quiet, but at the same time humming with a mystical energy. Caleb feels the great things that have happened here. He feels the growing presence of other great things that are about to happen, perhaps even to him. He doesn't know what those things will be. He only knows that they're coming.

Caleb will visit his mother's grave today. He'll go to the cemetery after the wedding. What will she say to him? He knows he'll hear her voice. Can he hear her now? He listens closely on the silent street.

Nothing. In a soft voice, he reaches out to her. "Mom?" But there's no answer.

Then he has a startling realization. He hasn't contacted the Reb, the great Kabbalist Elijah had told him about. He takes his wallet from the inside pocket of his jacket. The crumpled napkin is still there. The writing is messy but legible: "the Reb" and then a phone number.

A cafe is opening on the street up ahead. He hurries toward it.

It's not even eight o'clock in the morning. Can he call now? Yes, he has to.

Outside the cafe the owner is sweeping the sidewalk. "Good morning," Caleb says, and then in a hopeful tone, "Is there a telephone?"

"Yes, inside."

Caleb darts into the cafe. There's the phone. But he doesn't have any coins. He'll have to throw himself on the mercy of the owner. He does so without the slightest hesitation, because of how urgent this is.

"Excuse me, sir, I really need to use the telephone. It's an emergency. But I don't have any money with me . . ."

He makes a helpless, open-handed gesture. The owner smiles. "Don't worry about it," the owner says. He has not the slightest accent. He drops a few telephone tokens into the phone and hands the receiver to Caleb.

Caleb makes the call. After three or four rings there's an answer, the voice of an elderly man.

"Shalom . . ."

Caleb speaks in his broken Hebrew. "Hello, I'm Elijah's friend from New York."

"Ah, Caleb, I've been expecting you," says the Reb. Unlike the cafe owner, he has an accent. "I live on 18 Rechov Alkabetz. Can you come now?" He sounds pleased, not at all sleepy. "Can you come now?"

"Yes, of course."

"I'm so glad you've come to Safed. We can reveal holiness everywhere, of course, but this is one of the holiest places in the world. What street are you on?"

Caleb can see a sign on the corner outside the window. It's in Hebrew but he can read it. "I am at the Ari Cafe."

"That's good, very good," says the Reb. "Just walk until you see Ariel's bakery. Then go left to 18 Rechov Alkabetz. The second-floor apartment. One flight up. The second floor."

"Thank you," Caleb says, "I'll see you soon.

"Yes, God willing."

Eighteen Rechov Alakabetz is at the end of the block. Outside the building Caleb has a moment of doubt. How much of his plan should he reveal to the Reb? How much will the Reb know whether Caleb reveals it or not? Is he really seeking the Light, or is he letting himself be drawn into darkness?

Elijah had spoken of the seemingly random encounters that happen every day. Meeting Elijah in Times Square had been one of those encounters. Now Caleb is about to meet the Reb in Safed. Somehow that doesn't seem like a random encounter. If the Reb is really a prophet, he's someone who can converse with God. Perhaps the Reb sees things that Caleb doesn't really want to know, but that he's destined to find out.

In ancient times, a prophet could see the future. A prophet could show a person how to live righteously, and a prophet could also reveal the traps of negative inclinations.

"What will the Reb say about me?" Caleb wonders. He must challenge himself to find out. Holding a rusted railing, he climbs an exterior stairway to a landing on the second floor. Beside a weathered door painted white, a *mezuzah* is bolted to the door frame.

He knocks on the door and hears steps approaching. The door opens. There's a man with a gray beard but with youthful, gleaming eyes.

"At last, at last," says the Reb, with a warm smile. "Please come in. My name is Chaim. Or Reb Chaim. Or just Reb. It's entirely up to you. And you're Caleb?"

"Yes. I'm so glad to meet you."

The Reb steps aside and Caleb quickly touches the mezuzah, kisses his hand, and follows the Reb through a hallway, past a small kitchen, and into a living room that seems brighter than the rest of the modest apartment. Early morning sunlight is beginning to radiate through a pair of open windows, illuminating framed pictures of ancient sages on the walls. Floor-to-ceiling shelves are filled with leather-bound books with titles in Hebrew.

"Would you like something to drink?" the Reb asks. There's a pitcher of water on a credenza near one of the windows along with some rugelach, a pastry with chocolate that originated in eastern Europe.

"A little water would be great," Caleb says.

"And let's not forget the rugelach."

He pours water into an inexpensive plastic cup and puts rugelach on a plate for him. He places them on a low table in front of a leather couch, where they both sit down.

The Reb says, "Please recite the blessings out loud so I can answer amen."

Although Caleb is now used to mumbling the blessing with little concentration, as a child he was a blessing maven, an expert. He knew what blessings to recite for which foods.

He had even won a "bracha bee," the Jewish equivalent of a spelling bee for blessings. He recites the blessings slowly and clearly. He thanks God for the rugelach and the water.

The Reb responds with hearty "Amens!" Then he recites his own blessing, holding the cup in the palm of his hand and slowly speaking each word as if he were counting diamonds and rubies. Yes, this is a prophet. It seems to Caleb as if the Reb is speaking to God through the blessing in an intensely personal way.

Caleb answers "Amen" and the Reb drinks the water as if it were a gift from God. It's as though he'd never tasted water before. Then he smiles, acknowledging Caleb's presence in this very significant moment.

"Caleb," he says, "it's wonderful to welcome you to Safed, by the grace of God." He takes another sip of water. "Please tell me a little about yourself."

"Well, as Elijah may have told you, my mother passed away a few months ago. It happened suddenly, she was quite young, and it's been hard for me to accept." He pauses. "Her death was like an inner earthquake. I really feel out of place in the world and am only slowly finding an anchor and renewed faith.

The Reb repeats, "Out of place in the world. I've been there."

"Your parents died?"

"Yes, but not just that." The Reb continued. "I didn't mean to say, 'I've been there.' I should have said, 'I am still there,' because I can understand how you feel. Please continue, Caleb. Go on with your story."

"I feel like I've lost my bearings. My spiritual compass, if I had one. I grew up in an observant family, and I was never at all interested in following another path. I experienced a calling to be a rabbi but after my mom died, I felt angry at God. I can't understand how or why a loving God could do this to our family. I've tried to ask God for an answer. I've prayed about it."

"But God never responded, right?" the Reb says. "Most people have never heard God speaking to them directly. God doesn't appear out of thin air and communicate like I'm talking to you now. But that doesn't mean that God isn't present in your life. Sometimes, often, His presence is there in unexpected ways. The mystics teach that no encounter is random and if we are fully present we can experience God in any moment of our lives."

He continues, "In the beginning, God created an infinite light. The light was so powerful that the vessels in the world broke and this Divine light was hidden in all places and all times forever. As a response to the hidden light, God created humanity. You, me, every human being can reveal the hidden light at any moment. It may be through a blessing, a greeting to a stranger or a kind gesture. There is more. Sometimes we encounter moments when we are struggling with our faith or descending into places seemingly devoid of any holiness. This is a great challenge. In its own way it's a *higher* calling. It can be really heroic. Of course, it can also be tragic. It is no wonder that those who fall and rise assume a higher level in the Divine scheme of the world than someone who has never sinned."

He pauses, then asks, "Do you see what I'm trying to say, Caleb? Sometimes I feel like I'm not being clear."

"I think I understand exactly what you're saying. Sometimes only through descent can we elevate the most hidden of the sparks and grow stronger in faith?"

The Reb takes a deep breath. "Yes, Caleb."

Now he slowly rises from his chair and approaches the bookshelves across the room. With only the slightest hesitation, he selects a book and returns to his seat. As the Reb gently places the book on the table, Caleb is able to read the gold lettering on the cover.

"*The Secret of the Light*," he whispers.

The Reb nods. "Yes, this is a very powerful book. But like any book, its power is only available to a reader who is ready to fully grasp it and to use it correctly. We can even change negative energy into something positive. We can replace darkness with light. Or, rather, we can reveal the light hidden in the darkness . . . from the very beginning of time."

"Can we reveal the light in ourselves? In our own darkness?" Caleb asks.

"Of course."

"And we can also reveal the light in other people?"

To Caleb's surprise, the Reb doesn't respond immediately. His head bends forward, and Caleb can see that he's looking at the letters on the cover of the book. But then the Reb's eyes close. Has he fallen asleep? Possibly there's some health issue.

He turns the book around on the table, then slowly slides it toward Caleb.

"I want you to open it," the Reb says. "You have my permission. But before you do, I have something more to tell you, and perhaps this is the most important thing of all. Yes, I have one more thing to tell you."

"I want you to know that I do not know the ways of God. I can never tell you or anyone else why we experience tragedies in our lives. God's ways of reward and punishment are beyond human comprehension. Yet, when we experience pain or suffering such as the loss of your mother, we are faced with choices. Do we mourn our fate or create a new destiny? Do we lament the darkness or increase the light? Caleb, your mother was a holy soul who infused the world with so much love. Now that she is physically gone, you must fill the void with new light. She will live in you and through you always. Take the pain and live life with renewed purpose. If you are alive today, it means God believes in your power to heal the world that touches you. How does that happen? It may be something that is so small, easy, and insignificant that you overlook its importance. Or it may seem so large and difficult that you try to hide from it any way you can."

Now the Reb speaks in a quiet voice, but firmly. "Caleb, come closer. When I was eight years old, a great mystic informed me of something that changed my life. Even as a child, I had learned the concept of the thirty-six righteous people who sustain the world. Just like the physical world, the spiritual world can decay. It needs to be sustained by a foundation of kindness. The thirty-six people all over the world bear this responsibility and merit this blessing."

Now the Reb is speaking directly to Caleb's soul. He says, "Once I met the famed Reb Aryeh of Jerusalem. It was a brief encounter but unforgettable and his words are with me every day. Reb Aryeh was known as the Father of the Prisoners for his visits to the jails. His words brought love and compassion. Even the most stubborn prisoners responded to Reb Aryeh's love for his fellow man. He was also known for his visits to the sick, especially patients who had no family of their own. It was his practice to go to the hospitals of Jerusalem every Friday. First he would ask the nurses which patients usually received no visitors. He would linger with each of those people and bring words of encouragement."

Now the Reb raises his hand, as if to emphasize the importance of what he's about to say. "One day, when I was still a very small boy, I asked Reb Aryeh if he was one of the thirty-six righteous people who sustain the world. Then he put his hand on my head and looked into my eyes. He said, 'Maybe. Sometimes. Even if just for a few minutes. And, Chaim, you can be one of them too.'

"Caleb, God doesn't ask any person to be one of the thirty-six people every day and every hour. But each of us can be one of the thirty-six at any moment through an act of kindness that reveals the light. The choice is yours. Reveal the light or remain in darkness. The choice is yours!"

The Reb nods toward *The Secret of the Light*.

Caleb opens the book to the first page. He glances up at the Reb, then looks back at the book and quickly closes the book. He's obviously deeply affected.

He's about to pass the book back to the Reb, but the Reb's hand holds the book in place.

He says, "*The Secret of the Light* is a rare book. This one is yours forever."

At the wedding hall, rows of folding chairs have been set up. The chairs are higher quality than typical folding chairs. They're white, they have armrests, the seats are padded, there are eight rows of chairs with eight chairs in each row and an aisle down the middle. Eight is a positive number in Kabbalah.

Most of the chairs are filled when Sam and Nora arrive.

The guests, all strangers to Sam, turn their eyes toward him as he hurries down the aisle. He hopes he doesn't look as panicked as he feels. Where is Caleb? What is this absolutely gigantic mess with Maish about?

Today was a good dream and now it's turned into a bad one. He puts his hand inside his coat to see if the check is still inside his pocket. It is.

Danvers and Mouse are seated on the aisle toward the middle of the middle of the congregation. Danvers rises. "We've saved some seats. Where's Caleb?"

Danvers looks great, very well-rested. Mouse looks great too. They're in the spirit of things. But Sam looks awfully worried considering this a wedding.

"Caleb's on his way," Sam tells Danvers. "I'm sure he's on his way." He manages to smile at Mouse and then sits down. Nora is beside him in the special dress she brought to Israel for this occasion.

Now Caleb is there. He comes down the aisle so fast that he seems to have just materialized in the chair beside Sam. He's carrying a book.

"Where have you been?" Sam asks, peeved. He glances at the book. "Is that a wedding gift? It really ought to be wrapped."

Caleb is out of breath. He says, "Dad, I've decided to become a lawyer. I'll go to law school and then we can be partners in your firm."

Sam is thunderstruck. His jaw drops. He says, "I'm flabbergasted. I mean, I'm really happy. You've made the right decision. You can still learn Torah. You'll love the law."

Caleb shakes his head. "Actually, it is not loving the law but revealing the light in the law office that now energizes me.

I may not love every minute of it but that's why I'm going to do it, and why I have to do it. Torah will be my foundation and increasing the light in the world is my purpose."

Sam is confused by this. He feels a little punch-drunk. But the main thing is, his son is going to be a lawyer!

He takes the check from his pocket. "I want you to have the honor of writing your name on the payee line of this check. Here, I have a pen."

"Okay," Caleb says indifferently. He takes the check and the pen.

The whole thing with Maish hits Sam again. "There's some bad news about Maish."

"The gold chains?"

"You know about it?"

"Only that he sent money to Italy."

"They sent him garbage. He lost everything. His business is ruined. He has no cash. How is he going to meet his payroll? Also, he pledged a million dollars to the hospital in memory of Mom."

There's a stir among the guests as the ceremony begins. Yehoshua Gips is accompanied by his parents. The veiled bride follows as she walks down the aisle accompanied by her father on one side and her mother on the other, radiating joy. As the ceremony begins under the chuppah, Caleb's deep feeling of serenity makes him wonder how he could ever have come up with the apocalyptic scenario he had imagined. What had gotten into him? What kind of paranoid craziness led him to believe that Yehoshua Gips would get married to Orly?

Even if Yehoshua were to marry Orly, even if he were to remove that veil and Orly was standing there like the quintessential Jewish bride, Caleb would not have the slightest objection to that. It would be another chance to reveal the secret of the light.

As it happens, when Yehoshua Gips breaks the ceremonial glass and lifts the veil, it's not Orly who is revealed. It's another woman altogether, very attractive too but in a completely different way. Everyone in the room is on their feet cheering and applauding for the happy couple.

All this time, Caleb had been consumed with anger because he had thought Yehoshua was marrying Orly. In an instant, Caleb experiences overwhelming relief. Now he can truly join everyone in the room cheering and applauding for the happy couple.

Caleb is applauding too and shouting "Mazal Tov"!

Caleb turns towards his father and using *The Secret of the Light* as a writing pad, scrawls Maish's name on the payee line of the check. He hands it to Sam. He tells his father, "I will see you later." He rushes out of the hall. The light inside him begins to rise again.

Caleb finds the Old Cemetery of Safed. He doesn't look for it. He just finds it. The Old Cemetery simply appears. In the same way, Elyse's grave simply appears. He walks among the tumbled limestone grave markers, most of them white but some splashed with blue paint. He looks upward at the hill where the great sages lie. Then he's standing in front of Elyse's grave.

He kneels beside the grave. His right hand is buried in the dusty ground of Israel, his left hand holds the book. Once as a child he asked Elyse if God was real. "Of course," she said, and then with a laugh: "Don't ask silly questions." It was more than belief, it was a certainty for her. In Hebrew it is called *emunah*, the power that allows us to walk into the Red Sea and know the waves will part.

Caleb had never really felt that before, but now it's here. When the plane had taken off for Israel he'd spoken the words of the Twenty-Third Psalm, and now one of the verses comes to him with a new and startling certainty, as if the plane has landed safely and it could never have been otherwise. He feels a soft breeze, the wind, and knows that like the wind, he cannot see his mom, but she has never left him.

Suddenly, Caleb feels that someone is behind him. He senses the presence of Elijah. It's a shocking realization, as when Elijah had first come up behind him in Times Square.

He continues with the psalm. He says it aloud: "He restores my soul . . ."

"Oh, that's so sweet."

Caleb freezes. For a second he imagines it's Elyse's voice, but only for a second. He stands up and turns.

Orly is there, dressed as if for a company picnic in a red baseball jersey over a white t-shirt and a baseball cap. She's grinning mischievously until something in Caleb's manner takes the grin off her face.

"How are you? Are you okay?" she says, now full of concern.

Caleb steps back. "It's what you wrote to me. When I really want to see you, I'll see you."

"Yes," she says. "I knew you'd come here eventually."

"And you would be waiting."

"Yes."

She's very serious now, appraising, pitching her head as if to say, "Are sure you can deal with this? We'll see."

"Orly, I always hoped we would meet again. I felt an

instant connection with you. It is weird. Elijah was elusive when I mentioned your name after our first meeting.."

"Caleb, Elijah knew I was there, but he did not want to reveal my true identity until you were ready."

"What do you mean?"

"I was there on Elijah's behalf to test you. Faith grows through struggle. Questioning your beliefs awakens inner fortitude and latent potential. The real me is a believer, like you." Orly smiled deeply.

"Orly, I cannot wait for us to spend more time together. I want to get to know the real you. God willing we will deepen our connection."

Caleb continues, "An artist can reveal a beautiful letter on an empty canvas—not drawn onto it but drawn out of it because it's always been there. We can do that for each other because each of us is the canvas and each of us is the artist. We're also the letter, the *aleph* that's been silent and invisible, but not anymore. Every person is a spark of light, you and me, and we can reveal that light inside ourselves and in the world every day."

"But how are we going to do that?" Orly asks. There's an extraordinary look on her face, joy and sorrow, doubt and hope, or hoping for hope. And, even now, a tinge of sly humor.

"How are we going to do that, Caleb?"

"With this," he says, and with both hands, as if in a ceremony, Caleb presents her with *The Secret of the Light*.

But as she reaches to accept it, she stumbles backward. The book falls. He grasps her hand and then releases it once she is up.

Her eyes brighten. She glances down at the book. "Look," she says, surprised. "Most of the pages are blank.

What will we do?"

"We'll write it together."

Elijah and Caleb: A Few Weeks Later

As Caleb exits the bus, Caleb looks around the Western Wall plaza. The mystics teach that more than any place on earth, this area is the epicenter for seeing God and unleashing the hidden light in the world. The plaza is filled with the hustle and bustle of people young and old from all over the world running to catch the last rays of light at afternoon services and tourists learning ancient and modern history.

"Over here . . ." Caleb turns around and sees a man with sunglasses on . . .

"Elijah!"

Caleb turns around and recognizes Elijah beneath the shades. The sun setting casts a shadow on Elijah.

"Caleb, I am so glad you connected with Orly. We have known each other for a few years and she, like you, has chosen to embrace *The Secret of the Light*."

Caleb smiles. Elijah continues, "As I shared with you in Times Square, the primordial light is everywhere. Even in the darkest of places, the light cannot be extinguished. Every human being possesses the potential to unleash this light at any moment. Caleb, I am proud of you.

"I want to speak to you about something as my time with you is coming to an end . . . for now."

Elijah speaks with a sense of deep purpose like Caleb has never heard before.

"The words on the first page of *The Secret*, written by King David, are the most important and timeless message for revealing the light. If you can keep his words front and center every day of your life, you will tap into the highest frequency of living. Your mother will not only live in you . . . but *through* you."

> *To All Bearers of This Book—Always Remember:*
> *'Kol Haneshama . . . my entire soul praises you*
> *Almighty . . . Hallelujah . . .'*

"King David, who walked in the valleys of the shadow of death and scaled the peaks of joy, possessed the vision and strength to see God always . . . Tamid . . . Always, never wavering in his belief in the power and potential of every moment to reveal the hidden light.

"His final words in Psalms are his guide for all humanity."

Caleb now understands what his dying grandfather had told him when he was a child. "Tamid, Always," he had whispered to Caleb.

Elijah takes a deep breath as he looks into Caleb's eyes.

"I am not sure if you heard Caleb, about the ninety-three-year-old man in Italy who suffered from a debilitating virus that affected his ability to breathe. He was on a ventilator for one month. Thank God, he recovered. Upon leaving the hospital, he began to cry when he was given the bill for the one day's use of the ventilator. The doctor asked why he was crying. Was it because he couldn't pay the bill?

"What the old man said brought tears to the doctor's eyes. 'I don't cry because of the money I have to pay. I can pay all the money. I cry because I have been breathing God's air for ninety-three years, but I have never paid for it. It takes five thousand dollars to use a ventilator in the hospital for one day. Do you know how much I owe God? I didn't thank God for that before.'"

Caleb shudders.

"The entire soul . . . *Haneshamah.* The words for soul and breath in Hebrew are the same. Every time we breathe in and out is God's way of letting us know that He believes in us, loves us and that He is counting on each of us to reveal the hidden light. Our inhale is God's investment in us, and our exhale is our investment in God and our role in the world.

"Caleb, follow these four paths, ones you have learned, to align your life with the secret:

1. *Do Not Lament the Darkness, Increase the Light.*
2. *Reveal the Light in Every Moment.*
3. *Transform Obstacles into Opportunities.*
4. *Flood the World with Acts of Kindness.*

"The rest is up to you. Every human being is endowed with a unique role to reveal the hidden light unlike anyone ever born. The blank pages are our eternal impact on the world. The pages serve as a soul tracker for daily reflection. Set aside time each day to contemplate deeply on how at least one of these principles guides your life. Fill the pages of your book with acts of kindness, expressions of gratitude, and ideas for impact. Caleb, the opportunities are infinite!"

Elijah and Caleb have been sitting for a while in the large stone plaza area in the shadow of the Western Wall.

"Elijah, thank you so much for everything. I believe God sent you to me to help me, to light my path forward."

Elijah smiles a smile so deep it is as if he is waiting for

Caleb's words to trigger this response. "Caleb, I know you think that God sent me here to help you, but in fact as much as you needed me, I needed you."

Caleb's eyes open wider than before waiting for Elijah to explain.

"You know, on the day we met, I had returned early in the morning from a visit to Jerusalem. I am generally here a few times a year. I went on that trip because I was having my own crisis of faith."

Caleb looks stunned.

Elijah continues, "You see, when I was young, my parents revealed to me the meaning of my name. I will never forget when I was about ten years old, my father and mother told me about the prophet Elijah. They told me that his life mission was to inspire others to reveal their inner light and reveal the hidden lights in the world. My father said—and he repeated it often—'Be an Elijah.'

"He told me, 'Always remember that you may not be able to change the world, but you can change the world of one person each and every day.' My dad loved Mark Twain who said, 'The two most important days of your life are the day when you are born and the day you understand why.' Caleb, on that night in Times Square, I learned again why I was here. It was to guide you.

"As I was sweeping the streets that night, God sent you to reawaken my belief in my mission.

"Caleb, thank you. I realize my mission continues. Yours is just beginning. Never forget every human being is a potential Elijah. We are all tasked to spread the light. Keep *The Secret of the Light* close, reflect on it daily and practice one of the principles each day. It is the roadmap for you and all humanity."

Elijah lifts up his hands. "Caleb, I want to bless you. May God send His angels to watch over you every step of the way. May you walk in His light and illuminate the world."

Caleb answers, "Amen."

He feels his mother's presence and a renewed sense of his mission to bring light to the world.

As Caleb raises his head, he sees Elijah turning to walk away.

"Elijah," Caleb calls.

Elijah disappears in the crowd. Caleb knows it is not forever. Elijah can be anywhere and anyone. Everyone is a potential Elijah, and one more Elijah moment can be the catalyst for the redemption and the revelation of light throughout the universe. He will never forget the Divine gift of Elijah in his life.

IN APPRECIATION

I first met Rabbi Cohen several years ago when he became the pulpit Rabbi of BMH/BJ Synagogue in Denver, Colorado, a traditional congregation that many of my family attended over the past one hundred years. Rabbi immediately recognized my interest in the study of Judaism and philosophy and agreed to study with me in what I would call a nontraditional manner as taught at the Yeshivas.

Throughout our studies it was apparent that we both had a loss of a loved one that provoked many academic and philosophical questions that needed to be explored.

Rabbi approached me about writing a book discussing the ever presence of our loved ones, especially my mother and dad, and whether we are able to take comfort in knowing they are present now and whether we will be reunited in the hereafter.

The journey to have some type of proof other than faith was very important to me as I have grown older and I hope more educated in what Judaism teaches us about the mystical teachings of this important subject.

I challenged Rabbi to write a book in memory of my parents, Syril and Ethel Shraiberg, that not only academically but philosophically help us through the experience of living today and reconnecting with our loved ones.

After reading this book several times, I have gained much insight into the basis of why I am convinced that my loved ones are ever present. This book has given me an enlightened perspective of a real basis to believe in the everlasting soul. I am more confident now that I am surrounded by my loved ones.

The Secret of the Light not only will appeal to Jewish beliefs but is a basis for all religions and beliefs to assure themselves that our loved ones are always present.

—*Steve Shraiberg*

ACKNOWLEDGMENTS

I will never forget my first meeting with Steve Shraiberg over twenty years ago when he asked me whether he would reunite with his parents in Heaven. My answer in the affirmative launched a journey of friendship, learning and shared belief that the souls of loved ones are ever present in our lives. It is an honor to dedicate this book to the memories of Steve's parents, Ethel and Syril, whose souls continue to soar. I am grateful to Steve and Kay for their support, patience and belief in me.

The odyssey for this book took many twists and turns. No encounter in the process was random. A divine encounter at a funeral almost seven years ago set me on a path to meeting a mystic in Jerusalem who opened my eyes to the depth and power of the Book of Psalms as a roadmap to revealing God's light in all of life's mountains and valleys and in between. It changed my life and all whom I touched and serves as a testament that changing the world begins with changing ourselves.

I am eternally grateful to the members of Congregation Agudath Sholom where I serve as Senior Rabbi for your friendship, love, openness to sharing our life journeys and understanding that my cup overflows with blessing when I am renewed and refreshed.

Thank you to my agent Anne Marie O'Farell who truly pushed me to the limits by encouraging me to write about my encounter in Jerusalem as a parable. Thank you for your brutal honesty as the manuscript evolved and introducing me to Mitch Sisskind, to whom I am forever grateful and without whom this story would never have seen the light of day. Thank you to all of the people who supported me on this journey; you are truly angels in my life.

My mother, of blessed memory, lives in me and through me and together with my father, he should live and be well, instilled within me a never-ending spring of optimism, faith, kindness and life purpose that pulsate in the pages of this book. I carry in this book the love of them, my step-mother, Meryl, all of our children and grandchildren, Sara Malka, Avi, Aharon and Meir, Michal and Yishai, Adina and Moshe, Elisheva and Yaakov Moshe, Tamar and Feivel and Shalhevet and most importantly my soulmate and best friend, Diane.

Diane, words can never adequately express the depth of my gratitude and love for you. What is mine is yours and your support, wisdom, honesty, patience and truly inspiring me to do my best is beyond anything I could have ever imagined. God willing, we will be blessed to reveal the light in ourselves, our family, community and world for many many years to come.

CPSIA information can be obtained
at www.ICGtesting.com
Printed in the USA
JSHW011949240523
42194JS00006B/56

9 781946 928306